Introduction

Writing is, in my humble opinio
gifts. No other creature in the world, in the entire known universe (although I would be glad to be proved wrong on that count), has the ability to express itself in a way that others can enjoy, appreciate, relate to and connect with. While the same could be said of art or music, I believe that writing offers something unique, something that nothing else can give (not to knock either artists or musicians, of course). Writing has the ability to create new worlds, new people, cause disasters and heal wounds, break hearts and realise dreams. And the best part about it is that anyone can do it.

My love of writing began at an early age, from when I first started reading. For me, reading and writing have always gone hand in hand. You read books, and they give you ideas for your own writing. You write, and that makes you want to explore new ideas and themes by reading books. It is an endless literary circle of creativity and imagination, and one of the greatest self-fulfilling prophesies ever told.

At the time of writing this, I have attempted writing four novels, only one of which has been completed. The fourth is still in development, but first two have alas been consigned to the paper bin... for now. I do not regard the unfinished texts as failures, not like a painting with a half blank canvas or an incomplete statue missing it's head. I see them more as stepping stones, little journeys that have helped shape me into the writer I am today. They've taught me many things (admittedly not all of them good), and I hope that these first four will not be the last.

However, there are some stories that do not need the hundred thousand or so words that constitute a novel. Some are best told in twenty thousand, or ten thousand, or a thousand or, in some cases, as little as a hundred. These short stories are the focus of many competitions across the world, partly because they are so short. To tell a story in a short, concise way, keeping it short enough to keep the reader interested but long enough to build an engaging tale is a great art, and one that, alas, I am still a long way off mastering. But you can read my attempts at this art here, in my first collection of short stories. Some are brief, some longer. Some were for competitions, some just for myself. Some are descriptive, some are fast-paced. These short stories and the competitions that came with them have helped me grow my confidence in my writing, made me more willing to share it with others, and given me such great pleasure in the writing.

To all aspiring writers, I would encourage you to enter as many of these competitions as you can. They're a great way to gain some experience, meet interesting people, possibly even earn a little cash. Most of all though, they're a great excuse to just sit and write, to enjoy doing what you're passionate about. You may not win every competition you enter. And not everyone who follows my advice (to be honest, you might be wise to ignore it; I'm not renowned for my wisdom) will win competitions. But anyone who does follow my advice can win competitions. And to anyone who is feeling discouraged, I would say only this.

J.K. Rowling, one of the most successful writers of modern times, worth in excess of 650 million pounds today, was rejected by publishers 12 times when she first pitched *Harry Potter and the Philosopher's Stone*. Today, she's earning 72 million pounds a year, has one of the most dedicated fan bases in the literary world, and has had her books converted into billion-pound films (*The Deathly Hallows Parts 1 & 2* grossed over 1.7 billion between them). And while the stories themselves are excellent, I personally don't consider the writing to be outstandingly exceptional. Don't get me wrong, they're well written. But it is the stories and the world she created for them that have made her so successful, rather than the writing itself.

Anyway, I should go before I further alienate any Potterheads. Enjoy!

Strangers on a Train

The Tube carriage is the same as it always is; stuffy, sweaty, and suffocating. Overpriced, overdue, and overcrowded. Too many people in too little space, all breathing the same air, all thinking much the same thoughts.

Except me.

All these people, though they may not know each other, are connected. They are small connections, but connections nonetheless. They travel on the same train, every day, at the same time. They got into the same carriage. Some will even have gotten on at the same station. They will be travelling to similar jobs, and will live similar lives. Tiny similarities, barely worth noticing. But they are enough. Enough to mean they are not strangers to one another.

And they are not strangers to me. But I am a stranger to all of them.

The man by the doors, thickset, in a leather jacket and jeans, scratches his beard and yawns. His name is Mike Miller. He works in a butcher's shop, carving the meat, feeding it through the mincers, cleaning the knives. He takes up too much space, his six foot four build looming over the other passengers. The kind of figure that would make you cross the road if you saw him walking towards you at night.

Miller is also a single dad, a keen photographer, and an amateur poet. He has two small daughters named Charlotte and Rachel in his rented flat. In his spare time, he likes to travel out to the country and take pictures of the wildlife and flora. Yes, he may spend a lot of time at the gym. Yes, his appearance may lean towards the aggressive. But he grew up in the kind of neighbourhood where 'dog-eat-dog' was an understatement. And so, he made himself look as imposing and intimidating as he could. Not for offence, but to defend those he loved. He loves his two daughters dearly, loved his mother before she was killed. He is a good person underneath. Yet nobody cares to look beyond the surface. All they see is a glowering, powerful stranger.

In the seat next to mine is a severe looking, sharply dressed woman scrolling on her phone. She has an angular, school teacher face and black hair pulled back into a knot so tight that her forehead looks stretched to breaking point. Everything about her screams 'boring businesswoman'. Looking at Marlene Francis, you'd never know that she was the wife of the leader of the most ruthless drug gang in London, and that she was not only responsible for keeping track of the money, but had personally beaten or killed no less than six people who had made the mistake of crossing her husband. The documents she is scrolling through, though innocent in appearance, are shipping manifests for cargos of cocaine, details of the latest drug sales, and account details for corrupt coppers who are well paid to look the other way.

Stood between the seats, hand gripping the support pole tightly, is Grace Fenbrook. At least, that's her day name. She works in the Lickity-Lick ice cream parlour Monday to Friday, nine 'til five. The ice cream there isn't half bad. But, as soon as the shutters roll down and the bright, cheery space falls quiet, she swaps the pink dress and apron for something a little tighter and more leathery. She becomes Rose Nightingale. Her website, which opens with a striking photo of her in a half mask and corset, rather seductively promises "A place where dreams really do come true. No matter what they are..." I can't help but wonder if any clients have ever unwittingly brought their children to be served by Grace, and if they would let them eat the ice cream knowing where Rose's hands have been.

The list goes on. There are a couple of teenagers stood with their lips locked together, both seemingly enamoured with each other. The very epitome of young love. Wild, free and uncaring. And yet, both are cheating on the other. Both know it. Neither does anything about it.

Andrew, the cheery looking, round-faced man in the suit is in fact a divorced, depressed alcoholic. None of his colleagues know. And the bruises on that boy's face are not from the bike fall he talks about, but from his father's fists.

These people see each other every day. They know the faces, maybe even some names. They know where they get on and get off and when they can move to more comfortable positions. They do not know each other's secrets, but they would not call each other strangers.

Yet there are strangers on this train. Two of us. We are strangers to the rest. But only one of us is a stranger to the other.

I've bought meat from Mike Miller, and passed him on his countryside walks. I've posed as a buyer from Marlene Francis's husband, and, rather reluctantly, made use of Rose Nightingale's services. I did what I had to do. I've watched the two teenagers on their double dates, been to an Alcoholics Anonymous meeting with Andrew, and been forced to witness a father beating his son. But I had to do it. It's my job.

It's my job to make sure there are no strangers. None, except me.

And yet, here is one.

I have to give him credit, his appearance gives nothing away. He looks totally relaxed, the white wires of his earbuds snaking up out of his pocket, head nodding slightly to the beat. A backpack rests on the floor by his feet, the sleeve of a raincoat hanging out of an unfastened zip. He could be a tourist heading into the city, or maybe an office worker enjoying a day off. A faint shadow of ash grey stubble covers his chin, thinning and fading down his neck to his Adam's apple. His arms, exposed from the faded Guns 'N' Roses t-shirt, are tanned, toned without being overly developed. He has a defined, handsome face, a strong jawline partially hidden by the stubble, and attractive blue eyes.

Edward Vane.

They were right to send him for this job, even without knowing him. Strangers sending strangers. Though his good looks draw attention, they deflect thoughts away from why he might be there. His calm, relaxed demeanour lets him appear completely normal. A natural actor. Although he is a new face, he is not a suspicious one.

A perfect stranger.

But not to me.

I know who he is, even if the others do not. I know who sent him, even if he does not.

And I know what he's here to do.

To them, he is a stranger.

To me, he is a target.

A twitch. His eyes widening slightly, the pupils dilating just a fraction as the adrenaline begins to kick in. He's felt the phone vibrate in his pocket. His head stops nodding to the beat that isn't there. A hand reaches up to remove the earbud that isn't an earbud. He looks down at the backpack that contains something other than a raincoat and tourist supplies.

He's received the signal. Go time.

The train shudders and rattles along the underground tracks, moving towards the next station. Unless I act now, it will never arrive.

I'm on my feet even as the hand holding the plastic bud comes down. The pistol, previously hidden under my jacket, is out before I've straightened up, the cold eye of the muzzle focussing on Vane.

"Secret Service! Stay where you are. If you move, I'll fire!"

We'd received the tip-off of the incoming attack two weeks before. Nothing more than a date, a time, and the target of a train. That is why I know these people. That is why I had to watch them, study them, find out their secrets. I had to be able to identify the threat instantly, without the delay caused by eliminating possibilities on the spot.

As it happened, Edward Vane was known to us as a potential extremist. Say what you will about the Government's tightening of security, the invasion of privacy as some call it, but Vane wasn't the first we caught because of it and he won't be the last. When he boarded this train, I knew instantly that he was the target.

He's looking at me now, fear mixed with shock in his blue eyes. His hand is still clutching the tiny plastic device on the end of the wire.

Time slows. I can hear every beat of my heart, an eternity stretching between each one. The train has stopped moving. In fact, it's not even there. Nor are the other passengers.

The only things that exist are me and Edward Vane. The bomber and the spy. The killer and the protector. The devil and the angel.

Resolve.

I can see it harden in his eyes. He's resigned himself to his death. He might as fulfil his task, propel himself onto his journey to Paradise. The other passengers mean nothing to him. Their deaths will not bother him in the slightest. They are just strangers on a train.

He has his job. But I have mine. And only one of us can succeed.

Two fingers, on opposite sides of the carriage, each move half an inch.

This story will always hold a special place in my heart. It was the first piece I wrote for a competition, which was the 2017 Olga Sinclair Short

Story Competition. Based on the theme of 'Strangers', this competition, run by the Norwich Writer's Circle, was my first taste of competitive creative writing, and the first time I'd ever really shown my work to anyone other than my close friends or family. I don't know what inspired me, but I wanted to write something about how little people actually know each other, about how we can recognise people yet still be strangers to them. And about how, to some, nobody is a stranger. This was not the only piece I wrote for this competition, but it is the only one I was satisfied with. The other two, one about a hacker and one about a terror attack, both ended up unsatisfying and unfinished... for now. I wrote Strangers on a Train while I was on a World Challenge Expedition to Morocco, and, I will confess, part of it was a desire to impress certain members of my group. But I will never forget taking my notebook and pen up onto the roof of the school we were staying in, looking at over the dark and empty streets of Ouarzazate, and writing underneath the African stars. I have not yet found a better place to write.

Between the Devil and the Deep Blue Sea

Th nightmare began with a pair of swimming goggles. This is an unusual thing to kick off a catastrophe, I know. A secret meeting or an accident in a laboratory would be more normal. Nevertheless, a pair of goggles was what started this nightmare. For, without them, the dive would never have been made, the artefact would never have been discovered, and there would have been no nightmare.

The goggles in question were blue, plastic and rubber, with slight break in the seal of the right cup, meaning salt water kept leaking into the eye of the wearer. He rose to the surface, his blond hair breaking out of the water into the bright Mediterranean sun. Reaching down with his feet, he could just touch the soft sand carpet with his big toe, the surface pluming around the current he produced. Slightly walking, mostly swimming, he made his way back towards the shore, until he could rest his feet on the seabed with his head clear of the water.

The blond-haired boy pulled the goggles off his face, feeling the rubber elastic strap ping off the back of his head. Shaking them to empty out the water, he glanced around the little bay, a smile on his face as he took in the pleasant scene.

There were people everywhere, lounging on sunbeds on the sand, stretched out on airbeds being gently rocked by the waves, children ducking and diving and splashing around in the water. Above, the sun blazed, the temperature a hot but pleasant thirty-two degrees. Beyond a dividing rope, a small speedboat roared out to sea, an inflatable sofa dragging behind it. The four children on it shrieked in delight, their air-filled support bouncing over the wake. The sky was a brilliant blue, with only faintest traces of clouds that somehow managed to make it even more perfect. It was, simply put, paradise. If there had been someone from the Ibiza Tourist Board present, they couldn't have asked for a better day to photograph.

As the boy was strapping the goggles back on, something slimy and heavy burst from the water behind him, hurling itself at him out of the waves, its limbs outstretched, nails like talons reaching for his back. It crashed into him, arms wrapping around his chest. The boy lost his balance and tipped forwards into the sea, crying out in surprise. For a moment he was blinded, confused, unable to breathe. He let go of the goggles and they smacked backwards into his face, thudding into his brow. He thrashed wildly, trying to remove the slimy limbs that were encircling him. Then, he was forced to the surface and hurled forwards, landing face first back into the salt water. Feet finding the floor again, he turned to face his attacker.

"Lay off Mol." He half smiled, still spitting salt water out of his mouth.

"What's wrong Ben?" The girl grinned back. "Little sister overpowered you again?"

"You got me from behind, when I wasn't ready, and was distracted by these fricking goggles. Yeah, you really overpowered me."

"Excuses excuses." The girl jumped at him again, but he caught her this time. He tried to swing her around, but her arms, slimy with sun cream and seawater, slipped out of his grasp. In a flash, she adjusted her own goggles and plunged back under the surface. Shaking his head, Ben turned around, found the rope that encircled the swimming area, and struck out along it, a powerful breaststroke propelling him through the water. Beneath him, the sea seethed with life, the water so clear it might as well have been blue tinted air. A shoal of tiny fish, each one flashing in turn as the light caught them, shimmered beneath him, hundreds of tiny moving bodies. Larger, slower fish, coloured so lightly that they almost blended in with the sand below them, drifted along the seabed, moving lazily through the seaweed forests. A boat lay half buried in the sand, the hull split and cracked where some careless tourist family had landed it on a rock. The fish darted in and out of the wreck, nibbling on the plant life that had attached itself to the fibreglass surface.

Ben swam on, watching the bottom slope and descend beneath him. A baby squid, almost perfectly camouflaged, propelled itself across the sand, its tentacles rippling through the water. It disappeared among the seaweed, and Ben lost sight of it. He moved on, following the line of the rope until it cornered, marking the edge of the designated swimming area. He turned, and began to swim back along it towards the shore, watching the marine life drift and dart beneath him.

The swim was about a hundred metres there and back, and he was a little out of breath by the time he reached the beach. He sat in the shallows for a moment, enjoying the feel of the small waves breaking against his chest. He'd managed to pick up a slight tan without burning himself, and he was pleased to see his skin changed from its normal pale shade. A slightly larger wave broke over Ben's face, splashing up into his eyes, making him splutter. When his vision cleared, there was a man standing before him, water streaming off his pale chest, a kind smile playing on his lips.

"You alright Benno?" He asked, reaching down to ruffle the boy's wet hair.

"All good Dad." Ben replied, smiling back up at him.

"You seen the cairn?"

"The what?"

"Come on, I'll show you."

The two splashed their way down the beach a little way, passing a group of kids fighting over an inflatable unicorn.

"How're the goggles holding up?" Ben's father asked.

"They're alright." Ben shrugged. "One of them leaks a bit I think, but it's nothing too bad."

"I can take them back if you want?"

"Nah, they're working fine. Besides, you take 'em back, I wouldn't be able to do this." He grinned, hurling himself into the deeper water. Bubbles burst around him as he plunged below the surface, rolling onto his back to look up at his father's distorted face. He grinned again, and rose up.

"Here it is. Dive just down there." His father pointed down. Ben did so, swimming down to the seabed, peering through the murky water. It was harder to see here, the sand and other debris churned up by all the movement obscuring his vision. He wasn't exactly sure what he was looking for, but something pulled his eyes towards it. And he knew instantly what he was meant to be looking at.

It didn't look like much at first. There was a pile of rocks, heaped on top of each other, resting on the seabed. They were all different sizes, lumps of pumice lying next to marble pebbles resting on top of sandstone chunks. The pile was about a foot and a half wide, perhaps half a foot tall. Ben didn't know why, but something about it made him shiver. It was a perfectly mundane sight. It wasn't like he'd never seen a pile of stones before. But even so, there was something that didn't seem right about it.

He rose back up to the surface, gasping for breath as his head came out into the air. He'd been under longer than he'd realised. Turning back, he saw his dad standing nearby, watching him.

"Weird, isn't it?" He smiled. "Looks like somebody tried to hide something."

"Buried treasure maybe." Ben grinned. "We should dig it up. Release it."

A frown fell across his face. He hadn't meant to say that last bit. In fact, he didn't even remember thinking it. It was as if someone else had put the words in his mouth for him, and they'd just come out before he was aware of them. He stopped moving forwards, wondering what had happened. Then he realised; he didn't remember starting to move either.

"You ok son?" His father asked, looking slightly concerned. Ben shook his head, sending droplets of water sparkling through the air, tiny ripples spreading around him as they hit the surface.

"Yeah. Yeah, I'm fine. Just had a bit of a moment." He shrugged, trying to make light of it. "We gonna take the pedalo out then? Not got much time left to do it."

"Yeah. I'll go and book it now. I'll give you a shout when it's time to set out." Ben watched his father wade out of the water, brine cascading from his wet trunks. He hadn't noticed the strand of seaweed that had attached itself to the material, the slimy plant flapping lightly against the back of his thigh with each stride.

Ben turned back towards the – what had his father called it? A cairn. That was it. He ducked back beneath the waves, looking for the pile again. It wasn't hard to find. Once again, something seemed to guide his gaze towards it. He swam closer, trying to get a better look. Despite the fact that everywhere else the sunlight easily penetrated down to the sandy floor, the cairn seemed to be shrouded in darkness. And although the sea had been bathing in the rich heat of a Spanish summer all day, there was an unnatural chill in the water. Ben was reminded of looking at a grave. No, it was more than that. A tomb.

Startled, he pushed these thoughts out of his head. Where was all this dark depressing stuff coming from? He was on holiday in Ibiza for God's sake. He'd had an amazing three days so far, and he had another three to look forward to. It was just a pile of stones under the sea. How bad could it be?

He swam forward, and pulled at the bottom stones, shifting the support from under the pile. The rocks began to slide, tumbling over each other as he pulled more and more out. Then, the mound collapsed in on itself, the top stones falling inwards. Ben came up for air, his lungs straining. He'd been so determined to break up the pile, he hadn't noticed how long he'd been under the water. When he dived back down, he almost swallowed water as a gasp of surprise mixed with fear escaped his lips.

There was a skull sitting on the seabed, surrounded by the shifted rocks. The hollow eye sockets seemed to stare up at him, the mouth grinning at him with its gumless teeth. He felt a shudder run through him and he jerked backwards, desperate to get away.

No. It wasn't a skull. It was just another stone. A very white, slightly skull shaped stone, but a stone just the same. It was the goggles distorting his vision, that was all. He hadn't realised that the right one was filling with salt water again. Ben broke the surface, treading water as he emptied the goggles and took a couple of deep breaths. His heart was pounding in his chest, and he forced himself to calm down. Why the hell was he so on edge? It was pathetic, seventeen years old and scared stiff by a rock. He'd be checking under his hotel bed for monsters next.

Once more he swam down, determined not to get frightened this time. He reached down, and grabbed at the white object. It came away easily, surprisingly light considering it was about the size of a bowling ball. Now he was closer, he could see that the rock did look eerily like a skull. There were dents for the eyes, and a sloping, rounded top that could have housed a brain. Peering through the plastic lenses of his goggles, he noticed the marks the water had eroded into the surface. It was all scratched up, almost looking like someone had carved symbols into the top of the rock.

He tossed it away, watching it sink down to the bottom, the sand pluming up around it as it struck. Normally, he might have kept it as a souvenir. He had a bit of a thing for skulls. But, even as he'd touched it, some voice had whispered in his head that this was not something to be kept. He'd wanted to throw it away from the second he'd picked it up.

He surfaced and dived again, making for the centre of the stones, where the skull had been. His ears straining against the pressure, his hands scrabbled in the sand, digging through it. He didn't know why he was doing it. It was that same unspoken feeling that had made him toss away the rock. Somehow, he just knew he had to dig under here.

His fingers connected with something hard and flat under the sand. He dug more, trying to clear away the debris to reach his prize. It was wooden, he was sure of that much. Before he could completely uncover it, he felt a straining pain in his chest. He'd run out of breath again, and kicked for the surface, gasping as his mouth was wrenched open in a need for air. He had to stop doing that; he was going to kill himself.

Ben floated on his back a few moments, trying to get his breath back. Up above, a slight cloud drifted past the sun, filtering its rays momentarily before moving on. Ben turned over, and made one final dive.

This time, he managed to completely clear the sand, exposing what lay beneath. It was a slab of wood. Just a piece of driftwood, roughly circular in shape, the edges ragged and torn. All that for just a bit of junk.

Ben reached down and picked it up.

Every muscle in his body tensed as something ran through him, ripping through his body from head to foot. It was like someone had just connected him to a car battery. There was a moment of brief, blinding agony, and for just a second, he heard a terrible, indescribable scream of pain and hatred. A face, demonic, not human, flashed before him, the eyes alight with fire, the mouth a snarl of pure malice.

And then it was gone.

Snatched away in an instant, leaving no trace. There was just a piece of driftwood in his hands. Ben was left wondering if it had even happened. Already it was slipping away, disappearing into a fog through which he couldn't see. He was running out of air again, that was all. Lack of oxygen was making his brain hallucinate.

He kicked for the surface, still clutching the driftwood, not looking down at where the wood had been. If he had, he might have seen a hole, just a few inches wide, in the sand. The sunlight filtered down to the seabed, but seemed to stop at this point, leaving nothing but a circle, so black it could have been painted. Even as Ben rose, the sand poured into it, covering the opening.

The hole had been open for maybe five or six seconds, no more. But it had been enough. Enough to awaken what had been at the bottom of it. What had been there for thousands of years, sleeping, dormant. Waiting to be freed.

*

That evening, Ben sat on his hotel room balcony, a glass of iced cola in one hand, an open book resting on his lap. Looking out to sea, he watched the sun start to dip below the horizon, the golden rim just touching the water. As he looked on, it sank lower and lower, staining the waves canary yellow, then tangerine orange, then blood red. It was a beautiful sunset, and Ben was glad he'd been able to come out and appreciate it. His dad and sister were downstairs in the bar, but

Ben had found that he preferred to read alone. He was working his way through Stephen King's IT, the mammoth novel that had terrified a generation. Ben didn't scare particularly easily, but he had to admit that King was good at his job.

He reached out to pick up his glass again.

His hand brushed against the piece of wood.

He'd brought it back with him. He'd had to. Something hadn't let him just leave it on the bottom of the ocean, lying there among the fish and seaweed. Ben didn't know why, but he just knew that he had done the right thing. In the dying light, he picked it up and examined it again. There really was nothing special about it. It was just a bit of debris, a little splintered and battered but otherwise unmarked. The wood had dried out in the last of the afternoon heat, but Ben had no clue what tree it was from. His dad could probably tell him; he did a lot of woodwork. But beyond that, Ben didn't know anything about it.

'Because there's nothing to know, dumbass.' He thought.

And yet...

The hotel room door opened behind him, making him jump as it banged against the wall. Why did Molly always have to throw the door open like she was a hurricane? The natural disaster in question breezed into the room, followed quickly by her father. She dived onto the bed and stretched out, yawning as she caught sight of her brother through the open balcony doors.

"How's IT going?" She asked, getting back on her feet and stepping through the door.

"IT's good. Too scary for you." Ben replied. Molly huffed. Then she spotted the piece of wood.

"Oh my God, you brought that back?" She asked in disbelief. "Why didn't you just leave it on the beach?" Ben shrugged.

"Dunno. Just did. Problem?"

"It's just rubbish. There's hundreds of trees at home you can get wood from. Hell, Dad's got stacks of it in the garage. Get rid of it. It's grotty and grim and you keeping it is just plain weird." Ben shook his head again.

Molly marched forward, and seized the wooden disc. Ben cried out, lunging forward to try and grab it off her.

"What're you doing?"

"I'm tossing it off the balcony. It's junk, something off the bottom of the sea! It's like keeping a strand of fricking seaweed or something."

"Give it back!" Ben growled. They grappled, each trying to wrench it from the other's grip.

And then, it split.

The wood cracked right down the middle, the two pieces coming apart, one in each child's hands. Molly stumbled back, and sat down heavily on the tiles, eyes wide and staring at the wooden fragment in her hands. For a brief instant, Ben thought he saw something flash in the dull brown surface, as if there were a shard of glass buried within it. But he looked again, and there was nothing.

Molly was still sat on the tiles, unmoving, clutching the broken object. Ben looked down at the half in his own hands. He suddenly felt revolted by it. What the hell had he been thinking? Bringing a bit of sea junk back to the hotel like that. Molly had been right, it was just plain grim. He dropped it in disgust, and went over to his sister.

"Molly? You alright?"

Her head snapped round to face him, and Ben recoiled in surprise and terror. There was a dark fire alight in her eyes, a fury beyond anything Ben had ever seen before. The eyes he was seeing were no longer his sister's. They were an impossible green, filled with rage and hatred as she glared at him.

Then there was nothing.

Molly was looking up at him from the floor, her blue eyes filled with confusion.

"Ben?" She asked. "What just happened?"

"The wood broke," Ben replied cautiously, still unable to believe what he'd just seen. Or had he seen it? Surely that hadn't just happened. "You fell down. You didn't hit your head or anything did you?"

"Don't think so..." She frowned. "I feel weird though. My head's gone all foggy."

"Everything ok out here?" Their dad asked, stepping through the open balcony doors. He looked down and saw Molly on the floor, still clinging onto the half circle of wood. "What you doing down there?"

"She fell over," Ben replied, nodding at the bit of driftwood. "The wood broke when we were both pulling it. I think she might have knocked her head on something. Said she feels foggy."

"Let me have a look," his dad said, kneeling down beside Molly. He quickly checked her scalp, feeling for any cuts or lumps that might be coming up. "Can't find anything," he announced, straightening up. "But we should all probably get some sleep. We've had a pretty full on couple of days and tomorrow isn't going to be any different."

"Yeah, ok Dad." Ben said, extending a hand down to help his sister up. She paused another moment, then took it. "Jesus sis!" Ben exclaimed, snatching his hand back. "Your hands are boiling! Like fire hot." He looked down at his own palm, half expecting it to be red and blistered. "You sure you're ok?" She looked up at him, and her eyes were blank. Not just empty, but unseeing. She looked right through him, as if he were nothing but a drawing on a glass. Ben felt fear begin to grip his stomach in its icy fingers. They weren't the eyes of a teenage girl. They were the eyes of something old, something terrible, something dangerous.

He blinked, and once more Molly's eyes were her own. It was like some sort of cheap special effect in a film. One second cold and unfeeling, the next warm and a little confused.

"Yeah. Yeah I'm fine. I just need some sleep." She glanced down, and realised she was still gripping the wooden piece. She stared at it for a moment, then hurled it, with all her strength, off the balcony. Like a frisbee, it sailed through the air, through the trees that lined the hotel's boundaries, and out over the water. The hotel was built into the side of a cliff, just above a little cove where the beach was, and the disc slowly fell through the dying light, spinning gracefully, into the deep blue water. It splashed, and sank.

*

Later that night, as Ben lay in his bed, he had a strange dream. It was strange, because it didn't feel like he was dreaming. It was like some sort of half dream, where the rules of science and reality merge and shift and anything becomes plausible. In the dream, Ben watched his sister Molly rise out of her bed on the other side of the room. Her eyes shone red in the darkness, and black fire crackled around her head. Slowly, she moved through the room towards him, passing around the sleeping figure of their father in the middle bed. As she passed by Ben's bed towards the balcony doors, Ben realised she wasn't walking, but floating. More tongues of flame licked around her bare feet, which glided a few inches above the floor.

The balcony door slid silently open, but nobody had touched it. Molly floated outside, out of Ben's field of view. Ben thought he heard something, something like a whoosh of air. But already, dark tendrils of sleep were beginning to wrap themselves around him, pulling him back down into their dark and empty embrace.

*

At the same point that Ben thought he heard a whoosh of air from his balcony, a young tourist couple were walking along the beach below the hotel. They were American, on their first trip abroad together. Both were drunk, holding onto each other and giggling uncontrollably. They stopped at the water's edge, looking at the path the moon made on the sea.

"Come on baby." The man said, a thick New York accent slurred by the many beers he'd drunk. "Let's go for a swim." Without waiting for an answer, he began to strip off, unbuttoning his light linin shirt to reveal a hairless, muscular chest.

"You sure babe?" The woman asked, giggling some more. "It's getting a little late. Wouldn't you rather we go back to the room?" She giggled again, the intent in her voice obvious. The man laughed, dropping his trousers at the same time.

"Ain't this gonna be a nice way to warm up?" He drawled. He laughed again, and splashed into the waves, kicking up spray as he ploughed through the crests. He stumbled, tried to turn it into a dive, and face planted in the water. Breaking the surface again, he roared with laughter, turning to face his date on the sand. "Come on in Liz." He called out. "It's a bit of a shock at first, but it soon starts feeling great." Liz giggled, and began to undress.

The man, Paul by name, lay on his back in the water, staring up at the stars above. He'd never seen so many before. He picked out the well-known Orion's Belt, but all the others meant nothing to him. Astronomy had never really interested him.

As he was looking up, he though he saw something flash up on the cliff above him. He looked over, glancing at the rows of hotel balconies that lined the slope. As he looked, something seemed to take off from one of them, shooting up into the sky. Up and up it went, passing briefly over the moon, and disappearing into the darkness. Paul turned over, meaning to ask Liz if she'd seen it.

The words never made it out of his mouth.

Instead, a scream of agony took their place. Pain like fire had gripped his left lower leg, rapidly spreading up, past his knee and up into his thigh. It was as if someone had started boring into his flesh with an acid coated drill.

A second later, he screamed again, as pain consumed his left arm, starting at his wrist but flooding the whole limb. Then, everything was pain, explosions of agony bursting all over his body. Blood pumped out into the water. On the sand, Liz had frozen, having no idea what was going on. She could see her boyfriend thrashing around in the water, his screams piercing through the night. It was three in the morning; there was no one else around. The bars around the beach were shut, and there were no cars passing or helpful locals on their way home.

A shark.

That must be it. It came to her in a second. She hadn't heard of sharks off the coast of Ibiza, but it couldn't be anything else. If she could get to him, she could get it off him. What was it she'd read? Go for the eyes and gills, that was it. Short, sharp jabs.

She charged into the water, yelling out to Paul to hang on.

She'd not taken more than two steps when she started screaming too. She reeled backwards, losing her balance and falling onto the sand.

Blood was pouring from her foot, spurting out from a wound that she couldn't see. The sand was stained crimson, a glistening smear left as Liz tried to scramble away from the water.

And then, for an instant, she could see them in the moonlight.

The sea was alive with them, twisting and diving, all over each other, all over Paul, biting him, tearing at his flesh, writhing around him as his movements grew more and more sluggish.

It was like something out of a nightmare.

The pain in her leg had spread up through all her body. It was burning through her veins, passing up through her chest and up into her head. It was consuming her, enveloping her. It was all she could feel. She tried desperately to turn herself over onto her front, to drag herself towards the streetlights she could see no more than a hundred metres away. They might as well have been a hundred miles.

The lights, which had promised safety, had offered life, blurred, then dimmed, then faded.

*

Ben woke with a start, the memory of his dream jolting him from his sleep. He was breathing a little heavily, a faint trickle of sweat running down the back of his neck. His legs were tangled up in the thin bedsheets, and the sheet on his mattress had come untucked from the edges. He sat up, pulling his legs free, and looked around him. His father's bed was neatly made up, but he was nowhere to be seen. That wasn't a surprise; he frequently woke early to take walks around the surrounding area.

Ben looked past the empty bed, over to his sister. The memory of the dream, her bare feet drifting above the floor, flickered through his mind.

Molly was still there, sleeping peacefully, a half smile on her face as her eyes slightly twitched behind her eyelids. The balcony door was shut, and there were no burn marks on the tiles or the sheets.

It had been a dream. A stupid dream. That was all.

Ben picked up his watch from the bedside table and examined it. 7:13 AM. He normally wouldn't have been up for hours, and neither would his sister. He wanted to just lie back down, turn over, and let sleep take him again. But he knew any possibility of going back to sleep was gone now.

He got out of bed, and went out onto the balcony. It was a beautiful Mediterranean morning, the sun rising gracefully up out of the sea, the sky a perfect clear blue. Even though it was still early, the air was pleasantly warm, the smell of salt carrying in off the sea. Down below, the waves lapped at the golden sand, perfect white peaks gracefully tumbling onto the shore.

A shout drew Ben's attention. There was a crowd of people down by the water's edge, clustered together, looking at something on the sand. From his position on the balcony, Ben couldn't see what it was. But just looking at it, he felt a shiver run through him. Quickly, he pulled on some shorts and a white short-sleeved t-shirt, slipped on his flip-flops, grabbed the spare room key, checked his sister was still sound asleep, and hurried out of the room. The hotel corridors seemed eerily empty. It was early, but not so early that people wouldn't be about. The buffet breakfast was already open; Ben could faintly smell the blend of different aromas drifting up from the floor below. There should have been families bustling along the hallways, children playing in the stairs.

But there was nothing.

It was as if the entire hotel was holding its breath.

With a growing sense of unease, Ben descended flight after flight until he was on the lowest level of the hotel. From here, he took a cliffside path that zig-zagged down the rock face down to the sea level. It didn't register in Ben's concerned consciousness, but the path was completely devoid of life. No geckos scurried away from his footfalls, no birds or cicadas chattered in the trees. There was a heavy, dead quality to the air that only thickened the further down he went.

The five-minute walk seemed to take an age. Ben felt like he wasn't moving at all, just walking in place. And yet, before he knew it, his flip-flops were sinking into the soft sand, the waves hissing onto the hot beach just a few feet to his right. The crowd of people had grown, and even as Ben watched, a police car and an ambulance pulled up on the road at the back of the beech, uniformed officials already getting out. They ushered people away, shouting in Spanish and English, driving back the tide of people anxious to see what was on the sand.

The crowd dispersed under the instructions of the emergency services, and for a moment, Ben could see what they had been gathered around. But somehow, Ben hadn't needed to see it to know. Even on the balcony, he'd known what it was.

There was a young woman stretched out just clear of where the waves soaked the sand. She was lying on her front, handfuls of sand in her bunched fists. Ben could see the grooves in grainy surface where she'd tried to drag herself away from the sea. Her left leg was covered in blood, the white sand around her stained, a crimson flower that had blossomed around the body. In life, Ben thought as the medics rolled her over, she would have been beautiful. But as her face came into view, there was no life or beauty left. The skin was grey and shiny, the veins in her forehead and neck bulging out, too prominent beneath the taut surface.

As the ambulance staff finished turning her onto her back, Ben felt his stomach turn. There were two wounds in the top of her left foot, just above the arch, startling vivid against the surrounding skin. They were black with congealed blood, the flesh around them a putrid green, streaks of dark red creeping up her ankle and shin. Ben could see two trenches of red running from the wounds to the edge of her foot, as if knives had been dragged through her flesh. He turned away, feeling sick.

Further along the beach, a fifteen-year-old Spanish boy entered the water at a run, laughing as he tumbled over the waves and dived into the water. The salt water lapped over him as he surfaced, his dark skin breaking the surface into the morning sunlight. He and his parents always came to Ibiza in the summer, finding the seaside resorts on the mainland much less entertaining than the island's famed nightlife. He'd seen the crowd gathered at the water's edge at the other end of the beach, but it hadn't bothered him much. Probably some foolish Englishman who'd gotten too drunk and banged his head. It wasn't going to stop him enjoying a morning swim. He waved to his father on the beach, flashing a grin of beautiful white teeth. The man waved back, stretched out on a sunbed, a bottle of Estrella Galicia beer already open in his other hand.

"No vas demasiado lejos, Miguel." He called. 'Don't go too far away.' Miguel responded with a thumbs-up, pulled his goggles onto his eyes, and set out to sea with a powerful crawl. When the water was too deep for him stand with his head clear of the waves, he took a breath and dived, feeling his ears pop as he descended. His brown eyes scanned the sand behind the grey lenses. He'd spotted a baby octopus or something on the seabed around here the day before, and he wanted to see if he could find it again.

As Miguel swam, he noticed how strangely empty of life the surrounding area was. The clear water enabled him to see for a good distance in all directions, and there wasn't a fish of any kind in sight. None darted through the seaweed, none peaked out of the cracks in the sunken boat, none drifted along the bottom, nibbling the sand for food.

There was nothing.

No.

That wasn't true.

Something lay on the seabed, a heaped mass half covered in sand. Miguel couldn't make out what it was, and his lungs were beginning to cry for air. He rose up to the surface, caught his breath, and went down once more, his lean arms and legs pulling him through the water. His last view of the shore was his father, a tanned hairy belly hanging over his flower-patterned swimming trunks, sipping from the brown glass bottle. And then, he was gone.

Miguel felt his stomach knot as he drew closer to the lumpy thing, although he couldn't have said why. Maybe it was the lack of fish. Maybe it was the chill in the water caused by something other than a lack of time in the sun. Or maybe it was the shape of the thing he was swimming towards.

Miguel, clamping down on the squirming thing in his stomach, reached out, and took hold of the top of the thing. The sand plumed up around where his fingers touched, exposing what was beneath. But what really gave it away was the way the thing rolled over, the way the long, tanned fleshy thing that Miguel had grabbed lifted up away from the main mass. The boy recoiled, bubbles escaping his lips as he cried out in horror.

He was holding a man's arm, the muscular limb attached to a tanned shoulder. The corpse had rolled as he had pulled the arm, and the face was now looking at him through wide, staring, sightless eyes. What really made Miguel's heart start going a mile a minute was not the dead, unseeing eyes. It wasn't the way the arm floated limply when he let go of it.

It was the wounds.

The man was covered in them. Round, needle-like puncture marks, crimson against the white of his flesh. Chunks of flesh had been torn off completely, leaving ragged strips of skin and muscle drifting around empty, gaping holes. The man's throat had been ripped away, and there was an awful white flash of rib peeking out from his chest. Miguel felt bile rising up in his throat, hot and acidic. And yet he couldn't look away. He'd been gripped by a kind of horrified fascination, and he couldn't tear his eyes from it.

The head finished its lolling, the mouth dropping open as it came to rest. Miguel could see the man's tongue, black and swollen, resting in his jaw.

Something twitched in the gaping wound in the tanned throat.

By the time Miguel realised it wasn't a tongue he could see, it was too late.

Almost in slow motion, the thing launched itself, like a coiled spring, from the corpse's mouth. Miguel could see a striped, slender thing racing behind the hole in the neck, slithering up the oesophagus (or was it the windpipe?) as the creature lunged forward. And then, it had latched itself over his left eye, the goggle lens offering no protection, the plastic splintering. Pain like acid drilled into him even as blood mushroomed out. Miguel thrashed, pulling desperately at the thing that had attached itself to his face. The muscular, slippery creature twisted and squirmed in the water, his scrabbling fingers sliding helplessly off its smooth body.

He rose to the surface of the water, screaming as his head broke out, the writhing form never releasing its death grip. He could feel something like fire, worse than the pain in his eye, spreading through his head, burning through his body. The sea was now busy with early morning visitors, hoping to catch a full day's worth of sunlight and sea spray. Heads turned and mouths gaped as the boy thrashed towards the shore, his arms and legs flailing, but more and more limply and less and less effectively.

From his spot on the beach, Ben could see everything with horror.

There was a long, thin thing attached to the boy's face, squirming in the air. It was black, black as night, thin rib-like bands of white running its entire length. End to end, it must have been at least four feet long, thicker than a drainpipe, a twisting, coiling mass of shining, shimmering muscle. The arrow-like head was pure black, so dark that the eyes that Ben knew would be there couldn't even be seen. Its jaws were locked around the teenager's eye, and Ben could just make out the fangs, white as bone, sinking into his flesh. Blood poured out around the terrible wounds inflicted on the boy.

A sea snake.

Ben watched on with a sick stomach as the boy collapsed into the shallows, the previously clear water now rapidly turning red. Around him, people were screaming, pointing, some already trying to get out of the water.

But it was already too late.

Even as Ben stood there, not more than three metres from the water's edge, the sea began to boil. More snakes hurled themselves out of the water, lunging at people from out of the depths. Children disappeared under the surface, pulled down by unseen horrors, blood pouring upwards mere seconds later. Huge men in the tiniest of swimming trunks were failed by their gym-pounded, sun-roasted muscles as lumps of their flesh were torn from their bodies. The snake attached to the Spanish boy had pulled itself off him, taking his eye with it. The empty socket pumped more blood into the water.

The lucky ones died in the water, their arteries severed or throats torn.

Life played an even more cruel joke on the ones who thought they had a chance.

A girl, no more than six, pulled herself out of the sea just next to Ben, two ragged holes in the right side of her chest, matching ones on her back. She stared up at Ben with pleading eyes, looking to the older boy for help.

Then, she collapsed, screaming, clutching at her wounds.

Before Ben's eyes, black streaks spread from the marks, flowing along the veins below the skin, rivers of darkness running rapidly towards the struggling heart.

Venom.

Around him, others were falling as they reached land, the venom acting impossibly quickly. The sea had changed from clear, pleasant blue to a nauseating red, streams of crimson rising from beneath the surface. Ben rapidly backed away as a snake lunged at him from the shallow water, the muscled animal falling just short and landing, hissing on the sand. As it had hurled itself into the air, jaws open, Ben had seen its fangs. Four of them, two top, two bottom, each as wickedly long and sharp as surgeon's scalpels.

Ben didn't even bother trying to find something to kill the thing. Getting anywhere near it was suicide. Instead, he turned and fled, running parallel to the water, wanting nothing more than to get back up the cliff path and away from the sea. He'd be safe there. These things couldn't follow him on land, and they definitely couldn't climb stairs.

A gun blast of thunder made him jump out of his skin. He glanced up, and gaped.

What he was seeing was impossible.

Above him, the clear Mediterranean sky was being invaded by black clouds. Ben could see them racing in, faster than any wind could carry them, thick, rolling clouds, coming from all directions to meet directly above him. In less than ten seconds, a cloudless, empty sky had become a churning, heaving mass of storm clouds, swirling like a tornado, blocking out the sun for miles. Where there had been nothing but blue, there was now only black.

And then, something plummeted out of those clouds, faster than Ben could register, a streak of lightning that punched into the beach, sending sand erupting in all directions. Ben looked at where it had fallen, and froze.

It couldn't be.

It just couldn't be.

Molly was standing in the middle of a smoking crater, sand blasted clear around her.

But what Ben was looking at was not his sister.

At first glance, she was unchanged. Her auburn hair hung about her shoulders as it always did, her skin the deep brown it always went when she caught the sun. She was wearing the same turquoise t-shirt and checked shorts that she always slept in.

But this was not his sister.

For a start, his sister had never been able to levitate off the floor as she was doing now, rising up out of the crater like a vampire on a bad day. Her entire body was consumed by fire, black flames licking across her skin as she rose. Her eyes were no longer their pleasant sea blue, but a deep emerald, glittering with malice as she stared at him.

"Mol-Molly?" Ben asked without knowing why. This wasn't a teenage girl.

The thing that wasn't Molly laughed, a terrible, primal laugh that grated against Ben's ears like sandpaper. It was a sound that was older than anything Ben had heard, older than humanity, maybe older than life itself.

"Your sister is gone." It hissed. Its voice was raspy, choked, dry.

"What are you?" Ben demanded, rage giving him strength he didn't know he had.

"I have no name of my own." The Molly-thing replied. "I was once called Kituch Amoto by those who were here before. Those who betrayed me." The green eyes narrowed. "And now I will have my revenge."

"Who? Who betrayed you?" Ben yelled. Molly's face twisted into a sneer of pure hatred, and lightning flashed above them, the following thunderclap splitting the air like a sword.

"They called me here to help them!" Kituch Amoto howled. "They called me from the Beyond to save them. They promised to worship me!"

"Who?" Ben bellowed again.

"Those who were here before you! Those who existed at the dawn of humanity!" Came the snarled reply. "The Kifo Nyeusi plagued them. Hunted them. Killed them!"

"The Kifo Nyeusi? What do you mean?"

Kituch Amoto laughed again.

"Look around you, boy. You can see their power for yourself."

The sea snakes.

"They brought you here to kill the snakes?"

"They brought me here to use me!" Another flash of lightning sliced through the sky. "They wanted me to use my power to consume the Kifo Nyeusi. In exchange they would worship me like a God!"

"Consume? You eat these things?"

"No, you foolish boy!" The thing roared again. "I feed on the souls of all living things. Like this." A crack of thunder, louder than any that had gone before, bellowed around the sky. At the same instant, forks of lighting exploded from Molly's outstretched fingers, arcing through the air, passing just past Ben's head. He turned, and watched in horror.

He hadn't even been aware that there were still people on the beach. Reality had melted away into nothing but the standoff between him and this... thing that had possessed his sister. But there were still tourists and locals all around him, staring, terrified, at the scene that was unfolding. The lightning struck them, each one in turn, and burned them where they stood. More than that; each one became flames, any trace of human form dissolving in a heartbeat as they combusted.

The flames, a ghostly blue, flickered for a moment, shadows dancing across the sand. Then, each one compacted itself, forming a small, floating ball. They floated forwards, like will-o'-the-wisps, reaching the burning body of Molly and disappearing. Her head threw back, and the black fire around her leapt up, as if burning hotter. When Ben looked at where the people had been standing, there was nothing ash. He turned in horror to face Kituch Amoto, who was now grinning even more malevolently than before. Molly seemed to have grown taller, more thickset, the eyes shining even more green.

"What the hell are you?" Ben howled, outraged at the slaughter he was witnessing. On the sand around him, the last of the sea snakes' victims were beginning to still, the sea still boiling with the mass of venomous creatures.

"You would call me a demon." Kituch Amoto replied. "I come from where you would call Hell. But such labels do me no justice. I am so much worse than that. I am the Devil himself, young Ben. I cannot be defeated. I am here to end your world. Starting with you, and your pathetic sister."

"If you are so powerful, why didn't you destroy us all centuries ago?" Ben countered, the tiny traces of an idea starting to form in his mind. "You said there were those who betrayed you. What did they do?"

"They summoned me to help them." Molly hissed at him. "I consumed almost all of the Kifo Nyeusi, driving the rest away to be imprisoned. But then they turned on me. Trapped me in that fragment of sacrificial alter you so helpfully picked up, locked me in with a cursed skull. I was forced to lie, dormant, waiting to be free.

"But they did not leave the humiliation there. They could have killed me, but they would not! They spared me, only to use me further! Even in my dormant state, I could still consume the Kifo Nyeusi. So they used me to keep them contained. Imagine it. Me, a being of unimaginable power, being both imprisoned and used to imprison! They used me in so many ways. And so," She spat. "I will take their world in punishment."

"Cursed skull?" Ben asked, even as an image flashed through his mind. "That white rock in the cairn?"

"Yes, boy." The demon cackled. "I made you throw that away. Just lifting it from my tomb gave me enough power to influence your mind. And now it is lost, guarded by the Kifo Nyeusi. My old enemy, now helping me live. Isn't life poetic?"

A shout, a voice he recognised. Ben looked down the beach, and saw his father running along the beach towards him, kicking up sand as his sandals pounded down. He skidded to a halt beside Ben, gazing in horror at his daughter.

"Molly?" He shouted, as another thunderclap ricocheted around the bay.

"Dad, don't go any closer." Ben warned, as his father stretched out a hand. "She's been possessed by a demon." Amazingly, his father didn't even question him. After all, Ben supposed, with the amount of crazy shit occurring around them, this made some sort of mad sense.

"What have you done with my daughter?" He roared, his voice bellowing across the sand.

"Your daughter is mine." Molly laughed back. "And so is your world. Now choose, my friends! Kifo Nyeusi, or Kituch Amoto? How will you die?"

Molly began to float towards them, the flames leaping around her growing taller and taller. Behind them, the sea began to churn even more furiously, as the sea snakes sensed the prospect of another meal. The blood in the water had faded, but it was no longer the pleasant turquoise it had once been. It was now dark blue, so dark it was almost black. Ben and his father were being forced towards it as Kituch Amoto drifted forwards, arms outstretched.

They were trapped.

Caught between the Devil and the deep blue sea.

And then, out of nowhere, Ben began to sing.

He didn't think about it, he just did it. It was a song he and his sister had often performed together for fun, part of the talent shows they had done every time they finished a swimming camp in Mallorca. Master of the House, from Andrew Lloyd-Webber's Les Misérables. Ben had been the Master, Molly his wife. It had always been a bit of a joke, something they did because it had been cute when they were small and funny when they were older. They'd learnt the lines off a CD, and Molly had always been embarrassed to swear on stage in front of people.

And now he belted out those lines, those lines that he hadn't sung for three years, those lines that brought forward so many happy memories.

Molly stopped dead.

It was as if some sort of switch had been thrown, or a power supply had been disconnected. She just stopped moving, in an instant turning to a floating statue. Around her, the black fire seemed to falter and shrink, as if in a gust of cold air. The piercing emeralds of her eyes dimmed, hints of blue starting to appear at the edges.

The mouth opened, and screamed one word.

"HEEEEEEEEEEEELP!"

It was Molly's voice. Not some demon speaking through her, but his actual sister, still alive, still in there, still fighting for control. Ben knew that he would have only seconds. His singing would only throw off Kituch Amoto momentarily.

He knew what he had to do.

"Master of the House, Doling out the charm, Ready with a handshake and an open palm!" Screaming out the chorus at the top of his lungs, he charged forwards, grabbed hold of his floating sister, not caring where the flames flicked angrily around him, and hurled her forwards.

Into the sea, and the mass of waiting, writhing Kifo Nyeusi.

There was a scream of intense, incomprehensible pain and rage. The water around the demon was more snake than water, hundreds of them diving onto the thrashing form. Flash after flash of lighting light up the snakes as the demon tried desperately to consume them and save itself. But for every snake that was consumed, there were five more waiting to take its place.

Ben tore off his shirt and shorts and, despite his father's cries of horror, plunged into the sea. He pulled himself through the water, stroke after stroke, heading for where he knew it must be. He could hear the cries growing stronger behind him as the demon started to win the battle with its attackers. Ben dived desperately down, knowing it had to be near. But the sea was so black that, even if the salt had allowed him to open his eyes, he wouldn't have seen anything.

And then, his hand closed around it.

He didn't know how he could tell it from just a rock off the bottom of the sea, but somehow, he knew he'd found what he was looking for. Clutching it as tightly as he could, desperate not to lose it, he struggled for the surface, breaking into the air just as another clap of thunder crashed around him. Looking over, he watched in horror as Molly rose out of the sea, the last of the Kifo Nyeusi bursting into flames and being absorbed by the demon. The black flames reached higher than ever, dancing skyward as Molly left the water. Ben struck out for shore, his arms and legs thrashing as he willed himself to swim faster. He stumbled onto the sand, dripping salt water, and turned to look at Kituch Amoto. The demon was also on the beach, and heading right for Ben's father.

"You raised two brave children, old man." Molly hissed, the bite wounds inflicted by the snakes closing as she spoke. "You should be proud. At least die knowing that they would have tried to save you."

The thing in Ben's hand began to vibrate.

It wasn't shaking or rattling; it was buzzing, as if it had been filled with pure energy. Looking down, Ben saw that, as he'd initially thought, it was indeed a skull. The bone was pure white, but symbols had been deliberately etched into the surface. Somehow, Ben knew what they were.

Runes. Even as he watched, each one began to glow, a pulsing light emanating from inside the skull. And suddenly, everything became clear.

He drew himself up to his full height, holding the skull out in front of him, opening his mouth to call out to the demon.

But the voice that came out of his mouth was not his.

It was older, deeper, speaking in a language Ben didn't know.

Kituch Amoto recoiled, visibly flinching as the words echoed around him. It turned to face Ben, something in the emerald eyes that might have been anger.

Or might have been fear.

Ben continued forward, more and more light pouring out of the skull. Word after incomprehensible, alien word emerged from his lips, each one striking the demon like a hammer blow. The flames around Molly roared more fiercely, but their intensity was fading, as if the air supply was being decreased. Molly's feet thudded into the sand, and she fell backwards, scrabbling to try and get away.

"Fool!" Kituch Amoto screeched. "If you do this, you will never see your sister again! You can kill me, but can you kill her?"

Ben saw the lips move, but didn't hear the words that came from them. Golden light danced around him and the skull as he spoke the final few syllables, completing the ritual that would end Kituch Amoto, the being from the Beyond, once and for all. He could feel power, beyond anything he'd ever felt, flowing from the skull, flowing through him, flowing out of him towards his enemy as he banished him.

And then, just as he completed the unintelligible utterings, he realised what had been said.

He cried out in horror, desperately trying to reverse what he'd done.

But he was too late.

A scream, alien, unbearable, filled the air, tearing the very molecules apart as it ripped across the beach. It was filled with more pain, and more hate, than anything Ben had ever heard. Molly fell onto her back, head thrown skyward, mouth wrenched open. Steam seemed to be pouring form her eyes, her nose, her mouth, as if something was leaking out of her. Lightning tore the sky apart, the following thunderclaps almost deafening Ben as they punched into his ears.

There was a final, blinding flash from the sky. A bolt of light, moving faster than could be seen, struck Molly's prone body, sending it spasming on the sand, writhing, jerking. Ben ran forwards, falling to his knees beside her.

As he watched, the steam from Molly's mouth curled in the air, forming something that could have been a face, contorted in hatred, hanging over the sand.

And then it was gone. Blown away on the sea breeze.

The thunder stopped.

The clouds cleared.

In an instant, it was over. As quickly as the thunderous grey waves had rolled in up above, they were gone, retreating back over the horizon and out of sight.

The sun blazed back into light, the heat beaming down to warm the sea and beach.

Ben knelt on the sand, his sister's lifeless body in his arms. Her eyes were open, the blue irises empty.

Kituch Amoto was gone. But so was Molly.

Ben's head fell onto his chest, tears burning his eyes as they poured out, uncontrollable, unconquerable. He didn't hear the people clapping and cheering as they realised the danger was over. He didn't feel the sun's rays as they warmed his shoulders.

The skull that he had used to kill his sister lay on the sand behind him.

The empty eye sockets staring, the gumless teeth grinning grimly, as it watched the boy weep.

The story behind Between the Devil and the Deep Blue Sea is quite a strange one. Surprisingly, one of my most fantastical stories contains more reality than almost all of my others. I really did go on holiday to Ibiza with my father and sister, I really was reading IT by Stephen King, we really did stay in a hotel set into the side of a cliff above a beach. Ben's goggles were the same pair I was wearing on that holiday, right down to the leak in the right goggle. The description of Ben's swim and the marine life he saw is based off a swim I really made, and the beautiful Ibiza day was one I really stood and watched.

And the cairn was a pile of rocks my dad really found.

Everything that I wrote about that little discovery was true, bar the white skull in the middle of the rocks, and the hole in the sand. There was a little pyramid of stones on the seabed, they really did look like a tomb, and there really was a wooden slab underneath the sand beneath it. Admittedly, Mr King may have been having an influence on me, but my mind couldn't help wandering to the supernatural when I found it.

Sometimes, it's the smallest things that spark the biggest ideas.

Tom Brown's Cruel Days

Of course they did.

Of course they'd give me a question like this.

They just couldn't resist, could they?

Smug A-holes, sat in their offices, thinking the best way to screw over their hopeful students. They've got no idea what it's like to be a modern teenager, sitting modern exams, with the stresses of modern life and modern standards.

Discuss

What a stupid way to start a question. 'Discuss'. Discuss with whom? I can hardly lean over and start a conversation with the kid sat next to me; I'd get kicked out of the exam. And no matter how much I write, no matter how many questions I ask, the paper will never give me an answer back.

the techniques used and their effectiveness in creating a sense of foreboding

Techniques? The writer put some words on some paper. They told a story. Techniques? Shall I critique the way the letters fall on the page, their delicate, precise formation? In which case, you'd better provide me with the original manuscript, oh high and mighty teachers, so that I may properly analyse their writing techniques.

Of course, I know what they're really looking for. They want me to talk about alliteration, dramatic irony, sibilance, personification, the naïve narrator and that thing where the weather symbolises emotion. The pathetic fallacy, that's it. Not to be confused with pathetic phallusy, a condition that many boys in the year are often diagnosed with by their friends.

But their effectiveness? I don't see it. I don't get how people can look at this text and pull so many things out of it. Ideas of what the characters represent, of how certain words invoke certain images, of how a specific action is a foreshadowing of what's to come or the author's comment on society. I don't understand how people can say this is such a powerful piece, when all I see is words on a page. They just tell a tale. And pretty crap tale at that.

in this extract from George Elliot's *Silas Marner.*

Silas Marner. What a godawful novel. Don't get me wrong, I'm sure I could have enjoyed it. If I'd read it out of choice. If I'd been allowed to just appreciate it as a story and then leave it. If I hadn't been made to try and unzip it and pull out its literary guts for dissection. And as for this extract? It's one where bugger-all happens. Some woman who we were never really made to care about walking through the snow while high on opium carrying her illegitimate child in her arms. Sure, I feel sorry for the kid. Especially when the mum collapses and dies in the snow and the toddler is left stranded. But then, I can't help remembering, she's not real. She never was and never will be. How am I meant to emotionally connect with someone whose entire existence is fabricated? I have enough trouble doing that with real people.

Someone once said that your schooldays are the best days of your life.

Whoever said that, I got news for you: you're an idiot. Or maybe you just never went to school.

School is stupid; ask any fifteen-year-old. And I'm not just saying that because I'm lazy and would rather be at home on my PlayStation (although I did just get the new Call of Duty game, so that's not a half bad idea), or because I'm thick and don't understand it, or because I'm bullied and don't have any friends. Nothing like that at all, don't know what you're talking about, got loads of friends. Ok, my grades may not be the *best*, but I'm not exactly Danny Dumbass from Shit-For-Brains Street. But we're getting away from the point. School is stupid. Don't believe me? Alright then, why don't I walk you through an average school day? I'll show you just how crap it really is.

Since I'm in an English mock, might as well start there. We're looking at some Shakespeare play, Metre for Metre or something like that. All just a bunch of boring crap where nothing much happens. Although these lessons can be pretty entertaining, 'cause the whole play is full of sex talk. Who knew old Billy Shaky was such a horn-dog eh? It's always funny to watch Mr. Christian try and get through a scene without breaking down into a discussion of phallic imagery or innuendos for STDs. Speaking of old horn-dogs, Jack Christian is top of the list. There's a reason we call him Saucy C, and it's not because he likes his ketchup (sorry, bad joke). He's got to be eighty by now, but he still talks about sex like he's straight outta uni. He actually wrote a novel that was basically an erotica story (don't ask me about the plot, because I definitely don't know). When the school PSHE (that's Personal, Social and Health Education) teacher left, they brought Saucy C in to do the sex ed. while they found a replacement. I tell you, I never knew learning about a teacher's life could be so interesting.

Anyway, English is crap 'cause of essays like the one I'm sweating over now, and essays are stupid. Specifically, the word limits of essays. And I'm not talking upper limits, I'm talking lower limits. An essay is only as good as it is concise, right? So if I've concisely made my point in about a thousand words, why're you gonna make write another thousand words of crap? Ok, here's an exercise for you. In a maximum of twenty words, tell me what water is.

...

I said, 'Water is a colourless, transparent liquid that is found all over the planet, and which is essential for all life.' Easy enough, right? Now try and do it again but in two hundred words. It gets to the point where you don't even know what you're writing. I'd end up saying something like, 'Water can sometimes taste a bit funny, depending on what chemicals they put in it... Water makes things wet, but is not really wet itself, which means that something in water is not wet, but it is wet when you take it out of the water... Um... It forms the basis of urine.' You see? This is rubbish. It's unnecessary, superfluous, and uses too many words (yes, the irony was intentional there). That's why word limits are stupid.

Anyways, say we make it through the English lesson. Now, biology and history. These are two lessons that teach me absolutely nothing I will ever need to know. For example, I know from history that the Gunpowder Plot was in 1605, and from biology I know that there are things in cells called mitochondria that produce energy. Why the hell do I know this? It's never gonna be of any use to me. But while I do know these things, I don't have any idea how I'd go about getting a mortgage, or how I'd do my taxes if I decided to start my own business. No idea at all. But thank God I know the main newspaper headline from London four hundred years ago. Oh, and I've got that bloody awful pot I made in art class.

Someone's coughing. How inconsiderate. Don't they know there's people trying to procrastinate here? Just look round at this exam hall a minute. I'm just one of countless, huddled shapes, bent over desks, right arms (and some lefts) scribbling away on paper, left arms (and some rights) steadying their work. White shirts and blue blouses, navy jackets and crooked ties. None of us are alike. And yet, everyone seems to have found some common ground on which to write.

Except me.

How the hell do they do it? I wonder. Do words hold some hidden meaning to them that I am ignorant of? Does Elliot (or whatever the heck her real name was) captivate them in a way that I was never brought up to appreciate?

Maybe I was predisposed to hate this book. My dad studied it for his GCSEs (O Levels, as he still insists on calling them), and hated every word of it. When I told him I was doing it for mine, he laughed and said any chance I had of enjoying the next few years of English had just gone. He said the book was so bad, it had put him off reading for ten years. While I think he may be exaggerating just a little, I have to admit that even today I rarely see him pick up a paperback.

It doesn't help that so many of the teachers are so shit. I'm not kidding. I don't know how they keep getting their 'Outstanding' ratings from Ofsted. My theory is that Ofsted are so dumb that they actually tell the teachers when they're gonna be observed, so they'll go out of their way and spend like four hours planning the lesson, whereas they'd spend about ten minutes on the other ones. So normally the biology teacher Mrs Mycock (why the hell did she take her husband's name if it was Mycock?) teaches in one boring, lazy, monotonous way, but as soon as the Ofsted guy turns up, she completely changes. There's group activities, mini assessments, interactive PowerPoints, the full nine yards. Hell, she even talks different. It's incredible. And Ofsted are incredibly stupid for buying it. Listen up, Ofsted. If you really want to review teachers, surprise them for God's sake.

Don't even get me started on Mr Henning. What a miserable old knob. I genuinely don't understand why he's here. He's a grumpy old douche who clearly hates his job, and so his teaching is crap and we all hate him. I just don't get why he's still working in the school. He must have some sort of grudge against kids. Or maybe the headmaster owes him a favour. Sometimes I just want to say to him, 'Just piss off mate. Either piss off, quit, retire, or get fired man.'

And some of their responses, Jesus Christ. Here's an example situation from the history class.

"Excuse me, Sir. Can I go to the toilet?"

"Shut up and do your work Brown. You should have gone at breaktime."

Oh good. That old response, which, by the way, makes no sense. Break was like an hour ago. I'm asking you to go for a piss now. Also, get lost Sir. You're like sixty years old, you've got a gut that you're resting on the table. You've probably been constipated at some point in your life. In the same way that you couldn't go to the toilet whenever you wanted, I can't go to the toilet whenever I want.

Ok. Fair enough. I can go whenever I want. But to say that I should have gone at break is not a valid solution.

"What're you saying Sir? That the entire school should go to the toilet at break? That would be mayhem! So to avoid a potentially lethal crush becoming the norm, let me just go to the toilet Sir. Please."

"Shut up Brown! I said you should have gone at break."

...

Fine. Ok. Whatever Sir. You can give me a bullshit response that makes no sense and I'll just have to take it. That's not even the worst example. I'm sure you know the situation. You're in class and you've done something a bit stupid, like throw a paper aeroplane or something. The teacher goes,

'What do you think you're doing? What'd you do that for?'

And you say,

'Um... Ben told me to do it,' which, fair enough, is not a good reason. Then the teacher says,

'If Ben told you to jump off a cliff, would you do that as well Brown?"

WHAT? No, obviously not, you smartarse. Can you not see that a line has been crossed here between throwing a paper aeroplane, and leaping to my death?

Look up there a moment. Three rows up, one column to the left. The girl flicking her blonde hair over her shoulder, her hand moving smoothly across the page again and again, left to right, slowly progressing down the paper as she covers it in ideas.

Jenny Charleston.

God, she is so fit isn't she?

She's the only reason I tried at all in English, if I'm being honest. She's incredible at it, always at the top of the class, writing the best essays, reading more books than anyone should have time for. She doesn't even seem nerdy about it either. Exceedingly cool, strikingly funny, ridiculously good looking. I had to try. Couldn't let her think I'm just a complete dunce who can barely put pen to paper and who wouldn't know a subjunctive from a superlative. Couldn't let her think that. No matter how true it may be.

See that guy next to Jen? The scrawny, spotty boy writing like mad, hand untidily scrawling words in an uneven jumble. Matthew Tudor. God, what a pain he is. So smug, so smarmy, so good at abso-frigging-lutely everything. Especially English. It would be English that he chooses to really shine in. I see him across the classroom in lessons, sat next to Jenny, constantly whispering things in her ear, her politely smiling and occasionally laughing. Wish someone would just tell him to stick his whisperings, that Jenny would never even look at a freak like him.

Not that she'd ever look at me either.

Sports is what I'm better at. But don't get me started on PE and games. Jesus H Christ, who timetabled us to do badminton indoors in the summer, and cross-country running in winter? And has anyone ever actually cleaned out the spare kit room? I swear to god, even Ebola victims would rather stay at home than go in there. Plus, I'm not exactly the biggest guy around, so I don't really want to play rugby, because I'm gonna get murdered by some fat nobhead who's BO could knockout a skunk. But you need a permission slip to get out of it, otherwise the teachers basically throw you into the scrum headfirst and laugh as your ribs break. I swear, the number of times I've forged my dad's signature, I've become better at it than my dad.

So yeah. That's your glimpse into my school life. Pretty crap, isn't it? Like don't get me wrong, I think that we need schools so we're not all sat at home watching dickheads like Jeremy Kyle all day. But for God's sake, make them useful. Get teachers that can actually teach. Make us learn stuff that we're actually gonna use. And please, please, please, I beg you, for the love of all that is good and sweet in the world, send a guy with a biohazard suit and a flamethrower into the spare kit room.

Anyway, this bloody question. I gotta do this bloody question. So if you could just bugger off, I'd much apricate it. Thanks.

This is probably one of the more honest pieces I've ever written, despite it being much more tongue-in-cheek than some of my others. When I set out to write this story, I wanted to recreate your average teenager's internal monologue when he's sat in an exam that he hates. Like Between the Devil and the Deep Blue Sea, there are bits of this that are directly pulled from my own life and experiences. I did study Silas Marner for GCSE English Literature, as did my dad. We both disliked it, and my dad really did claim that it put him off reading for ten years. I really wanted to recreate the kind of sarcastic, exasperated air that most teenagers will feel when made to do something they don't understand. And then, of course, there are all the problems with school in general that I wanted to highlight and voice (although, admittedly, a lot credit must go to the YouTube content creator GradeAUnderA for providing a lot of my inspiration). The unnamed protagonist here, irritated by a text he doesn't like, distracted by a pretty girl near him, annoyed at all the things he finds stupid about school, is a character I think most young people will be able to relate to.

A Pirate's Life

The cannonball passes so close to my face that I can very nearly smell the traces of gunpowder that still cling to its smooth metallic surface. The missile whistles past me, passing over the far gun rail, and soars further out to sea, landing among the waves and disappearing. The air around the two ships is being torn apart, not just by the cannonballs and grapeshot that are being traded back and forth, but by the sounds that hammer at you from every direction. From ahead, the enemy ship's cannons roar, one by one, a battle cry that sends more and more mortal messengers my way. From behind, the crashing and churning of the waves as they chew hungrily at the sides of the ship, hoping to tip her over and swallow all of us aboard, to devour us in their icy depths and grind our bones to sand. The flashes of lightning that split the sky above are accompanied by the gunshots of thunder that threaten to cut you down with an almost physical force. The deck beneath my feet shudders, the sounds of the cannons below the planks bellowing up as they spit flames towards the opposing ship. Captain Rackham screams his orders from behind the ship's wheel, his normally deep and terrifying tones almost lost in the cacophony of noise that surrounds him.

The rain pounds down, each drop like the lash of a cat-o'-nine-tails as it hurls itself from the clouds onto my skin. The wooden deck is soaked and slippery underfoot, the crew members around me clinging desperately to ropes, rails, each other, anything they can get their hands on to stop themselves being thrown overboard as the sea mercilessly batters the boat, throwing it from side to side with each monstrous wave. The bombardment from the other ship's broadside isn't helping matters.

We should have known not to try and take her on. It was madness. She is a frigate, and we a humble brig. Not that there's anything wrong with The Falcon's Call. She's a fine ship, strong and sturdy, fast and furious. Her twelve-foot iron-clad ram protruding from her prow is the terror of smaller ships, her twenty-four-gun armament unusually heavy for a ship her size. Her crew is fast, efficient, and deadly. Her captain is one of the finest sailors to ever grace the waters of these West Indies. Any other type of ship would have stood no chance, her hull splintered and torn from our relentless broadside bombardments, her crew picked off by the expert precision of our swivel guns.

But not this frigate.

She's British, a Royal Navy warship, under the command of King George the Second. Her masts tower above ours, her deck rising a good three metres higher than our own. When the waves don't lift it up still further that is. We may carry twenty-four guns, but she carries almost two thirds of that on a single side. Her hull is thick and sturdy, her sailors steadfast and unafraid.

I can see her Captain, his sword drawn and raised above his head, rallying his men from the top deck. I can almost hear the words he calls to above the storm.

"To arms, men! To arms! They don't stand a chance. Send the pirates down!"

Of course, I don't need to hear them.

I've heard them before.

Once, it was I who stood on the deck of a frigate, my own sword drawn, looking down at the smaller boat whose men had decided to test their mettle against the might of the Royal Navy. They had barely made it past the railings before they were cut down.

Now, I look up at the larger ship, reflecting on how, one day, one of the men up there may find themselves in my position. Forced to turn their backs on the king they once swore to serve, because they realised he didn't care. Made to resort to piracy in order to try and earn a decent way of life. Will he feel the same guilt I felt at first, the betrayal of his king, his country? Or, like me, will it fade after the first prize, when he realises how much better life can be when he sails for the Gentlemen of Fortune and relaxes with the ladies of leisure?

I stagger over to the steps that lead up to the deck where Captain Rackham stands. An imposing, intimidating man, towering over all but the tallest of comrades and enemies, his blood red coat soaked in the rain, he still manages to maintain control of his vessel despite the furious storm that wrestles with him.

"Cap'n!" I shout above the roaring of cannons, crewmen, sky and sea. "We can't hope to sink them, Cap'n! Their hull's too thick, and their broadside will tear us to pieces before we can send her down. We're gonna have to board her, Sir! It's our only hope."

Rackham looks down at me, his eyes filled with determination and resolve. And something else. Something I've never seen before.

It's hard to tell in the flashing of the lightning and the stinging of the rain against my eyes, but it could almost be fear.

"Aye. You're right!" He yells back, the howling wind almost snatching his words away before they can reach me. "You lead the boarding party, Lad! Throw the grappling hooks, haul her in tight, and get up there. Tear those bastards to shreds!"

"Aye aye, Cap'n!" I turn, lean over the steering rail, and yell out to the crew, who are still spread out over the decks, the salt water washing around their ankles as they try to stay aboard. "Cap'n's orders! We're to board her! Grappling hooks away, arm yourselves up, and let's pull 'em down to Hell, lads!"

There's a cheer from the crew, adrenaline and bloodlust starting to kick in. The deck becomes even more of a hive of activity, as the sailors unlash the grappling hooks and begin to fling them skywards, the barbed hooks catching over the railings of the larger boat and digging into the wood. Muscles strain to pull the ropes taught and wrap them around the winch wheel, the ropes almost stretched to breaking point as the two vessels are pulled together.

"You!" Rackham bellows from behind me. I turn to face him. "You take the masts. They're sure to have shooters in the sails. Take them out." I salute him.

"Understood, Cap'n." I sprint down the slippery stairs, dodging round a crewman who's passing round cutlasses to the waiting pirates. On the deck of the frigate, the enemy crew are trying to cut through the grappling ropes, swords swinging again and again as they hack at the lines. It won't matter. We'll be on them before they can cut themselves free. I spring up onto a box at the foot of the mast, grab hold of a hook, kick down on a lever, and feel the thrill of exhilaration coupled with the savage wrenching on my shoulder as the winch releases and I soar upwards to our fighting top. A brawny, raggedly dressed sailor with a musket is crouched on the platform as I release my hold on the hook and land on the wooden surface, nearly losing my balance and plummeting back down again as another crazy wave rocks the side of the ship. I just hope the falling bag of sand that brought me up doesn't hit anyone on the way down.

"How's it looking?" I yell to the lookout above the cannon fire, which still bellows around us as the ships draw ever closer together.

"Got at least two rifles up in their rigging." The man yells back, his hand trying to cover the powder chamber of his weapon. "Their powder might be too wet to shoot, but I wouldn't count on it."

"I'm gonna go across and try and take them out. Cover my back."

Taking a quick moment to judge the distances, I sprint forward and throw myself off the platform towards the opposing ship's rigging. I'd never be able to make a landing on the swaying sail boom; the constant rolling and rocking of the two ships on the waves would mean I'd never make it. Instead, I jump spread eagled onto the rope net, tangling my arm in the fibres to stop myself falling down. For the second time in as many minutes my shoulder screams at my, joint being wrenched in its socket. But I cling on grimly, knowing my crew are counting on me. If their riflemen are allowed to just pick us off, we stand no chance.

Like some sort of giant spider, I scuttle upwards, heading for where I can just see the barrel pointing out over the platform. It seems luck is on my side; nobody saw me make the jump, and the rope, though soaked with rain, is thick enough to give me a good grip. Someone once told me that there was one sign of a true sailor that everyone missed.

"'s all in the 'ands and climbin', ma boy." He'd grinned at me over his tankard. "You watch a good sailor climbin', you'll see. Every finger's a fishhook, tha's 'ow you can tell." Well, it seems my fishhooks are good and sharp today. I reach the platform with ease, poking my head over the top and catching a glimpse of the scout up there, taking aim with his rifle. He hasn't seen me. Good.

I reach up, lock my fist around his ankle, and yank it forwards with much of my considerable strength. The man cries out, his rifle falling from his hands and clattering onto the planks he was standing on. He overbalances, stumbles backward, and plummets off the platform, screaming until he collides, head first, with the deck below. I can't hear the crunch, but I can imagine it.

Quickly, pulling myself up over the edge of the fighting top, I grab hold of the fallen rifle, check the powder, and put a musket ball in the direction of the other scout. He'd been perched on a similar platform on the mizzen mast, doing his best to take a shot at our crew. My shot doesn't land, but then I wasn't expecting to. With a weapon like this, even over a short distance, when I'm being thrown haphazardly about and so is my target, my hitting him would have required a minor miracle. And I never was religious.

It's enough to make him flinch though, turning and slipping on the wet planks. At the same time, the ship lurches again, and the mast slams forward as he falls back. His head rebounds off it, and he falls like a sack of tobacco.

My crew has begun the boarding by now, and it's clear that this fight will be a short one. With their untouchable scouts taken care of, the remaining British sailors lack the experience and ferocity that our men tear them apart with. Hand over hand, I descend the rigging to them, and am soon in the thick of it myself. A Brit rushes me, his blade flashing in the lightning, ferocity in his eyes.

I put a single shot from one of my four pistols into his chest, dropping the empty gun and drawing my sword. He stumbles backward, reeling, until he collides with one of his crewmates, and they both go down. Dashing forward, I drive my sword down, through the corpse and the man underneath trying desperately to shift the (quite literal) dead weight on his chest. My cutlass, the curved blade as sharp as a conga's tooth, slides through the sandwich of flesh and intestines that the top man has become, and easily continues into the second man. The point digs into the wood of the deck, and sticks there. I don't bother trying to pull it out. Instead, I draw two more of my pistols, and fire both in opposite directions, my outstretched arms momentarily turning me into a man-sized T with a smoking crosspiece. Two more British sailors fall, blood splashing onto the deck and mixing with the rain and salt water.

That's when I see the captain, cutting his way through our sailors, his wrist deft and agile as his sword dances through the air. Two come at him from opposite sides, one with a dagger, the other a sword of his own. The captain easily sidesteps a thrust from the dagger, parries the neck-level swipe from the cutlass, headbutts the wielder and slashes at the chest of the dagger holder as he tries to come around for a second strike. In the same smooth movement, he plants a firm kick in the chest of the reeling swordsman, sending him tumbling over onto the slick deck. A swift stomp to the throat from the captain's fine leather boots finishes him off. I know a true blade master when I see one. The way his sword is almost an extension of his arm, the grace and ease with which he dances across the deck, centre of gravity low, eyes never still, perceiving every threat before it appears and countering it with devilish ferocity. A skilled warrior, at home on the battlefield, one whose blade has tasted much blood and who is keen to feed it more.

I put the shot from my last pistol between his eyes.

That's enough to make the other Brits stop. Those with sense throw down their weapons and surrender. They know they don't have a chance. They're sailors, not soldiers. They can handle a cutlass and fire a pistol when they need to, but they're not trained in fighting. They don't have the endless brawls and skirmishes that we do to draw upon. They fling their swords to the ground and kneel, hands on their heads.

Captain Rackham stalks towards the kneeling prisoners, triumph lighting up his face.

"Gentlemen," He roars. "Hear me. My name is Captain Rackham. I offer you a choice. Join us, on our life of pillage, plunder and pleasure... or die here, on your knees."

The captured Englishmen look at one another, unsure what to do. Then one, a small, rat-faced man, stands up. He tries to look defiant and brave, but we can all hear the fear in his voice.

"I took an oath," he says, fighting to be heard over the waves that are still crashing and rocking the ship. "That I would serve my king to my death. That I would kill every last pirate that I ever met, and that I would sooner die than become one of them."

"So be it," Rackham replies, puts the muzzle of his flintlock beneath the man's chin, and blows his brains out. The body crumples, falling in a shapeless heap to the soaked deck. "Anyone else?" He enquires, casually reloading the pistol.

The Englishmen are staring, open mouthed, at the scene in front of them. Maybe they can't believe the reckless bravery of their crewmate. Maybe they're praying that their souls will be granted passage to heaven for dying for their King and Country. Or maybe they just can't believe the nonchalance with which our captain just killed an unarmed man in front of them.

Finally, a tall, broad man with a magnificent beard gets to his feet. He towers easily over Captain Rackham, who is by no-one's standards a small man.

"I too took an oath," he mutters, a thick Scottish accent resonating with bitterness. "But King George never cared for me. Never cared for my people. Never cared for any of us!" He gestures round at his crewmates. "He leaves us out here on a petty wage, letting us starve while the captain grows fat on the profits." He glances at the body of the man I killed. His tricorn hat has fallen from his head, the feather sodden and sagging. "I never liked him. He was a good sailor, a good swordsman. But he never gave a damn about how we were. He was just concerned with filling his own boots. For every shilling we earned, he got six hundred." The Scotsman spits onto the deck. A ray of sunlight slants down onto him, cutting between the sails and rigging. The storm is finally clearing, the clouds beginning to break up. The bright shaft illuminates the figure, almost deifying him. He resonates determination and power. "Whole goddamn navy's the same. Well, I've had enough. I think it's about time I earned a decent way of life, and took something from those who have forced us to accept the worst." He looks back up at Rackham. "Aye, I'm with you." So saying, he tears off his coat and casts it down onto the deck. "Cap'n." He salutes.

"Welcome aboard," Rackham grins.

It seems to be the tipping point for the remaining crewmembers. One by one, they all stand and throw down their coats. We suffered heavy losses today. Our ship is damaged and leaking. But we can repair and rebuild. Our ranks are bolstered. We will be strong once more.

Rackham walks over to me. "Good work from you, Lad," He bellows. "Fine fighting."

"Thank you, Cap'n." I reply.

"I lost my First Mate in the fighting. Care to fill the position?"

"Aye, Cap'n." I grin, saluting him. This is quite the day for me, it seems.

"What's your name, boy?"

"Teach, Sir. Edward Teach."

This one of those stories that I wrote because I just wanted to really. There was a driving force of a competition behind it, but I never entered A Pirate's Life into it. It was a historical fiction competition, but really, it was just an excuse for me to write a pirate story. Every boy is fascinated by pirates, by the life of plunder and adventure that Johnny Depp introduced us to. And, I'll admit, my interest was stoked more than a little in recent years by a certain game that I have spent probably too many hours playing. This is, of course, a highly romanticised view of pirates, as the reality was that they were more like businessmen than the rogues that we think of them being. However, the romanticised view makes for far better storytelling, and I just had to work Blackbeard being Blackbeard into there at some point.

The Man Who Isn't There

He's always there.

You know Him, but you don't *know* Him.

He's always been there. For as long as there's been a creaking under your bed or footsteps on your landing or a flicker in the corner of your eye. Always just out of sight, vanishing the instant you look for Him.

A nameless, faceless man that nobody knows, but everyone sees.

Of course, you tell yourself you don't see Him. He's not really there. It's just a trick of the light that you see, mice in the attic or some tectonic disturbance on the other side of the world that you hear. There's no-one there really.

There can't be.

Of course there is.

It wasn't a trick of the light that made your rocking chair start to swing when you were a child, the wooden frame creaking with laughter as it tipped back and forth, back and forth, back and forth. It wasn't mice that made you feel like the Venetian mask hanging on your wall, bought as a souvenir from a school trip, was watching you with its hollow eyes.

It was Him.

You never lose Him. Not really. You see Him more as a child, when the world is big and scary and you never really know what's going on. He is there, in every shadowy corner of your bedroom, down the dark flight of stairs to the basement, hovering inexplicably outside your window, pale face peering through the glass, watching you as you sleep. You don't lose Him as you grow up. You just become better at pretending He isn't there. You tell yourself not to be so silly, that everything has a logical explanation, that science can give the answer to what you're feeling. You're just overtired, overworked, not had enough to drink, had too much to drink. You're imagining things. Science can explain it.

Science can't explain why your eyes snap open for no reason in the middle of the night, your sheets soaked in sweat but you skin covered in shivering goosebumps. Science can't explain what makes the hairs across the nape of your neck rise when you walk past that stretch of woodland on the way home at night. Science can't explain that dark form at the edge of your vision.

You know it's Him.

You've always known it's Him. You tell yourself, time and time again, that He's not real. There are no flickering shapes in the corners of your eyes, you imagined hearing those sounds. Your explanations for the signs don't convince you anymore, so you pretend you never even noticed those signs. They didn't happen.

Of course they did.

You know they did. You just pretend they didn't so you can sleep.

Sometimes He looks different. Sometimes He's not just a shape, not just a figure. Sometimes, He's a jealous ex-lover come for revenge. Sometimes He's the school bully looking to hurt you again. Sometimes He's the monster from that horror movie your parents told you not to watch but you did anyway because you wanted to look cool in front of your friends and then made you not able to sleep for weeks.

He did that.

He's the reason you couldn't sleep.

In a way, you were half right. Science can explain some things. Science can explain, for example, that the reason you can't fall asleep is because adrenaline is pumping through your veins, preparing you to fight or fly, getting ready to face the danger.

It can't explain why you can't see the danger. It can't explain what the danger is.

Different cultures give Him different names. Different stories call Him different things. Everyone has their own name for Him. No-one can agree on one term for Him, even though everyone knows Him.

But then, how could they agree?

Nobody talks about Him.

You can't talk about Him. People will laugh. People will think you're paranoid. People might even start to worry about the state of your mental health and then they'll call the men in white coats who'll take you away and lock you up in a dark room and everything will start to unravel because it will be just you and Him and you and Him forever and ever and ever and no escape and no release and you and Him and Him and you.

Stop it, you tell yourself. Nobody's going to lock you up. You don't talk about Him because He doesn't exist. He never existed, not to you, not to anyone. He's a children's story, something to keep the little kids in line when they won't go to bed. He's not real.

Of course He is.

No, He's not. There are no flickering shapes hovering at the peripherals of your vision. There are no creaking floorboards under your bed, no eyes watching you from behind the window.

Then why have you got goosebumps?

Why, when I mentioned the Venetian mask hanging on the wall, did you shudder slightly?

Why, when I talked about the men in white coats, did your pupils dilate slightly and your heartrate quicken?

You know He's real.

You've always known He's real. You tell yourself again and again that He's not, each time hoping that this will be the one you believe, the one that will make it alright. But there is no Placebo effect that can touch Him. No matter how much you tell yourself He's not real, no matter how many explanations you come up with to quiet every screaming nerve in your body, you always know He's there.

He's always there, always watching, always waiting.

No-one knows what for. No-one can say who He is, where He came from, why He is here.

All you know are these two things. He's real, and He's scary. He fills you with childlike fear that you thought you'd outgrown.

He's there, and not there. Tangible, yet untouchable. Seen, but unseen.

You know Him. You've always known Him.

And you can never escape Him.

Ok, ok, this is a little different to my normal kind of thing. Being honest, I don't really know where the inspiration for this came from. Probably from reading too much Stephen King, but we'll leave that. This is, in my humble opinion, the best piece I've written to date. I guess the thing that I like so much about this story is that it's relatable to everyone. That's what makes it so scary. Everyone has their own personal bogeyman, their own thing that scares them when they're alone in the dark. We all get that feeling that we're not alone when we hear noises in the night. We all try and explain them away. I suppose I just wanted to play with the idea that maybe, Just maybe, you're right to be afraid.

The Art of the Kill

Killing is the easy part.

Everyone thinks it must be so hard. Forcing yourself to squeeze the trigger, knowing that doing so will result in someone's death, that you have robbed another person of life, that you have committed the most unnatural thing in this world, that their families will have lost a son, a brother, a father. They think that this must be the hardest thing about it.

It's not.

Killing is the easy part. It's not getting caught that's hard.

Which is why it's so much fun.

This particular kill, for example. I don't even have to worry about feeling guilty about ending another man's life. Not that I've felt that for years anyway. But this particular man, I would never have felt any guilt for killing. A drug dealer, a rapist and a killer, famed through the slums for his brutality and lack of compassion. It was positively pleasurable to put that bullet through his head.

Of course, a lot more went into it than that.

I had to track him. Follow his every move, learn his routine, record his habits. I had to know where he was going to go before he did, predict what he was going to do before it had been decided. Smuggling the high-powered sniper rifle into the city, finding a suitable vantage point, making my way to the rooftop (which involved picking several complicated locks and dismantling a sophisticated security system), all these things were challenges on their own. Each was all the more enjoyable for being so.

But the real fun was the steps I took to avoid being caught.

In a way, I consider myself a kind of magician. Although a much better one than those stage fools with their cheap special effects and illusions. Which ones of those grandiose, pompous tricksters can disappear as easily and effectively as I? Who among them can become invisible at will, so that no-one, not cop or crook, civilian or CCTV camera, can see them? And my tricks involve not smoke and mirrors, but solvents and make-up.

Sometimes, I'm not even sure what I truly look like. At least, not naturally. But that's not surprising. The face that looks back at me from the mirror is not my own. It has been altered, transfigured, enhanced and reshaped so many times that it's true form has long since been lost. And that's before I even start putting the make-up on.

Plastic surgeons are kind of magicians too.

I'm not sure anyone really knows me anymore. That's the simple truth of it. Any friends I ever had have long since disappeared, died or departed from me, and my idea of a relationship is a call girl I like enough to use more than once, and who's a good enough actress to pretend she isn't disgusted by me. It's not that I'm particularly hideous. That wouldn't suit the job at all. Sticking out like a sore thumb due to grotesqueness is rarely conducive to remaining undetected. No, it's me, not my appearance. It's the job. You don't even have tell people for them to detect something is different about you. It's like undertakers. They have a certain whisper of death about them that makes you shudder. Somewhat appropriate, then, that I should provide a steady stream of business for them.

But, I'm getting side-tracked.

My magic tricks.

Oh, I have so many.

Let's limit myself to just the ones I employed for this job. First of all, my skin. You can see it's a kind of olive tan, very common here in Rio de Janero. Perfectly even, head to foot. Thoroughly natural looking. But, this colour came not from the sun above, but from the little plastic bottle below my hotel room sink.

Well, that's not very impressive, I hear you say. Anyone can go out and buy fake tan at any corner pharmacy. Well, that is true. But how many corner pharmacies will give you a fake tan that you can remove in minutes with a little bottle of solvent? How many give you one that will last for weeks without needing topping up unless you remove it with aforementioned solvent?

Next, look into my eyes. Not above the eyes, not below the eyes, not around the eyes, in the eyes, as some of those petty illusionists might say. Muddy brown, small irises, unattractive. But watch, in amazement, as the brown turns to green as I pass my fingers over my eyes. The contact lenses disappear as my real eyes peak out at you.

I've seen colour changing contact lenses before, You scoff. I thought you said you were above cheap parlour tricks? Ah, but I am. You do not seem to understand that none of these things are any good on their own. They are not individual tricks. They are separate components of one grand illusion.

My hair. Go on, give it a tug. Real. 100%. But this dark, messy mop is about as far from my usual colour and style as a crumpet is from a croissant. They are both delicious savoury snacks, but the similarity stops there. Behold, as I empty this bottle over my head, and my hair magically becomes blond again. Bottle blond, you might say.

Yes, ok, that's pretty impressive, You admit. But surely that's not all you do? Not at all, my friend. Just reach inside my mouth, would you? Don't worry, I brush thoroughly. And, voila, there you are! These little inserts give me a cheekbone structure that most women would die for. If only they knew how easy it was.

But there's more. One final illusion that must be broken.

Take my jacket off me. Don't worry, that's all I intend to take off. This jacket is slightly too big for me. This is deliberate. Because, under my shirt here, I have a compacted spinal brace, which alters my posture, and small amounts of padding that alter my physique. My shoes have specially moulded soles that alter my walking pattern.

Do you see?

How can the police track down a black man when he is fact white? How can the mob hunt a man with a limp when he walks perfectly normally? How can my enemies send someone after me when I do not have the overdeveloped build they think I have?

I am a man without face. Without appearance. Without figure.

I'm simply a shape in the night. Disappearing as the first sirens sound.

The Art of the Kill was born out a long-held fondness and admiration for professional assassins that I harbour. While, of course, I do not condone their work, I do think that people underestimate how much goes into eliminating a high value target, and especially how hard it is to remain uncaught when doing so. Admittedly, I have very little knowledge of this myself as, thankfully, I've never met a professional assassin. A lot of my knowledge is second-hand (a big 'thank you' must go to Tom Wood and his Victor the Assassin novels; I can wholeheartedly recommend that series). However, I feel that I was still able to capture the essence of the transformation, and indeed the loneliness, that a contract killer goes through for each job. How would it feel to look in the mirror, and know that nobody, not even you, knows who the face looking back at you really belongs to?

Darkness

Lights.

Flashing, fading, blurring, blending. Red, blue. Red, blue.

Silence. No sound. No noise.

Shapes. Moving, right, left, near, far.

Darkness.

A face. His face, smiling.

Trees. Green leaves, green grass.

Birds. Singing. Chirping above.

White. A dress. A daisy. His hair.

His voice. Soft. Gentle. Familiar. Comforting.

"So, how about it?"

His eyes. Blue. Beautiful. Blissful.

No answer. No need. His face moving closer, eyes closed.

Moving through. Green darkening. White dimming. Birds fading.

His face like smoke, twisting and fading into nothing.

Darkness.

Sirens.

Loud, piercing, wailing, painful.

Pain.

Everywhere. Pain. My arms, legs, chest, head.

Darkness.

A beep.

Another.

And another.

Cool air. Chilled, artificial.

White sheets. Blue uniform.

"I'm so sorry. There's nothing we can do."

Words from nowhere.

Her face.

A faint smile.

A hand, trembling reaching from under sheets.

Fingers around a wrist.

"Be brave Mary. Be brave for me."

The hand loosening. The face relaxing.

Still. Thin. Tubes pushed into her.

Eyes empty. Unseeing. Unknowing.

One last smile, pink lips in white skin.

Pink darkening to red. Red filling to black. White fading to nothing.

Darkness.

Glass.

On the tarmac. Twinkling blue and red. Shards, like teeth. With glistening crimson saliva.

Suffocating.

No air. Can't breathe.

Darkness.

An engine growling.

Green blurs. Trees. Bushes. Grass.

Grey ribbon, white dashes.

A smell. Warm, dark, pleasant.

Coffee.

Hard, stiff, curving leather in hands.

Music. A man's voice. A song change.

Upbeat, happy. Rhythmic.

A buzzing. A tinkling sound.

A glowing screen.

His name. Black pixels against white pixels.

A fumbling. One hand tapping the screen.

A shriek. A horn.

A black shape, bearing down. Shining eyes, roaring voice.

Falling.

A voice. No words. Can't understand. Just noise.

And pain.

Everything is pain. My neck, back, fingers, toes.

Leather beneath my fingers. Soft, smooth, cold.

Lights. Blue, red, blue, red. So bright. Too bright.

And then.

A white light.

There is no noise. No hurt.

Just her face. His face.

Then, all is black.

Darkness was my first foray into flash fiction, and I must admit that I was quite pleased with it. Described by one of my friends and critics as 'the kind of stuff English teachers drool over', the original 100-word piece was my attempt at recreating the disjointedness and confusion that would follow a car smash up, or any kind of major accident really. I really enjoyed writing the broken up, non-coherent structure, and the challenge of keeping it within 100 words meant I really had to focus what I was doing and make each word count. It reads a bit like a piece of poetry, which isn't what I was going for, but which I don't feel is a bad thing. After the competition I wrote it for closed, I then went and extended the piece into the final version featured above. While this does somewhat defeat the point of the flash fiction element, I felt like there was just a little more I could do with the story to reach its full potential. The result is the piece you just read. It's a bit depressing and a bit dark, but that's one of the things I like about it. After all, when all's said and done, darkness is the only thing that always remains.

Strangers on the Street

The figure walking towards her shouldn't have been scary.

He shouldn't have been, but he was.

She couldn't put her finger on why, but there was something about him that made her bones shudder, that made the hair on the back of her neck rise.

There were things about him that could be considered intimidating. He was taller than her, for one thing, probably about five foot eleven. And broad, wide shoulders and a thick trunk. He wasn't exactly skinny and wimpy, but he wasn't a hulking brute of a figure either.

In a way, that made it worse.

His head was hidden by a hood, but as he opened his mouth, expelling white vapour into the frigid air, something flashed in the streetlight. Braces, fixed over his teeth like train lines, catching the light and winking at her.

It was a kid, no more than about seventeen by the look of him.

But in a way, that made it worse.

There was a dog at his side, a big one, the lead hanging limply from the boy's hand, a thick black cord that looked like it was designed to hold back something strong. The dog's heavy breaths misted just as the boys did, the clouds proceeding them into the pools of light that spilled onto the tarmac. The breaths were heavy, almost laboured, as if the creature was weak and unfit and it was an effort just for it to move.

But in way, that made it worse.

There were things working against him too, though.

For a start, there was what he was wearing. A blue and white jumpsuit style affair, the kind of thing that the kids were always lazing around the house in. As he passed beneath one of the streetlights, she could make out a word stitched across the chest in the white lettering:

TARDIS

She almost wanted to laugh. The TARDIS, from Dr. Who, the show adored by geeks and nerds everywhere, and it was scaring her. It was ridiculous.

The dog, too, wasn't a scary breed. It was no growling Alsatian or hulking Pitbull, but a bouncy, fluffy thing that might have been some sort of poodle cross. A labradoodle, maybe.

As he drew closer, she could see a lock of hair slipping down from under the hood. Golden blond. That was something she'd noticed before. It was very difficult to be intimidated by someone who had long, blond hair. Skinhead white, maybe. Not curly blond.

He shouldn't have been scary. He was a kid, with blonde hair, in a Dr. Who onesie, walking a fluffy dog. Yes, it was dark, almost half past eleven, and yes he might have been a little on the more developed side, but that didn't mean she should automatically stereotype him as one of *those* teens.

So why was she suddenly shivering? Why had she instinctively wanted to cross the road when she saw him approaching?

Maybe it was the way he seemed to completely disappear in each patch of darkness, phasing in and out of existence, almost the same way the actual TARDIS did on TV. Here one second, melting into nothing the next.

Maybe it was the way he walked. He barely seemed to be touching the pavement at all, his feet appearing to skim over the surface. There were no footfalls, no up and down motion as he took each step. He moved like liquid, spilling and flowing over the tarmac towards her.

Or maybe it was the fact that his breath was misting in the air on a June night.

She forced herself to keep walking. She was being ridiculous. She was scared because she'd seen too many news reports about violent youths and gang crime. But there were no gangs in this sleepy little village. He wasn't going to hurt her. Just look at his dog, which was even now trotting happily along, eyes twinkling.

Ten metres away.

Now five.

The air was cold, goosebumps racing over her skin. Her own breath was clouding now, the thick steam blowing back in her face as she walked.

"Good evening," she said, politely, trying to keep her voice from trembling. They were just two people from the same village passing each other on the street.

"Indeed it is," the boy replied from under his hood. His voice sounded old, much older than seventeen. There was a harsh, grating quality to it, like bones being scraped against each other. "Indeed it is," he repeated, looking round the streetlight-lit street. "Yes," he mused, and she noticed that he seemed to drag his 's's out into what was almost a snake's hiss. "A particularly fine evening."

She tried to step past him, but found her path blocked by the dog, which looked up at her with bright eyes, tail wagging happily.

"Where are you off to at this time?" The boy asked. His eyes peered out from beneath the blue cowl, and she shuddered. The eyes seemed to pierce right through her soul, almost sucking it right out of her. She turned her gaze back to the dog, reaching down to pet it.

"I was just coming home from a friend's. She lives on the other side of the village."

"Ah. How nice."

"Does she have a name?" She asked, still stroking the top of the dog's head.

"He. And yes, of course he does. They call him Barghest."

"Barghest? What an... unusual name."

"He has other names."

"Oh. I see." She looked down at the dog. Somehow, the eyes didn't look like a dog's eyes. They looked human, too human, shining with intelligence and understanding.

And something else.

Something that might have been excitement. Or anticipation.

"Well, it's been lovely to meet you and... Barghest," She mumbled, aware only now that she was shivering. "But I really must be getting home now."

"Ah. I'm afraid that I can't let you go just yet," The boy rasped, his voice like sandpaper in her ears. Maybe he smoked a lot. Her heartrate, already elevated, jumped up another notch. God, she'd been right after all. He *was* one of *those* teens. Any second now, something silver would flash in the streetlight from out of his hand, ready to lunge forward into her stomach if she didn't do as he said. Was this just a mugging?, she wondered, or did he have more sinister designs on her? God, why hadn't she just walked past him, why had she had to say hello?

"L-l-look," she said, trying to stop her voice shaking through her chattering teeth. Her whole body was trembling now. "I don't have any money on me. I don't even have my handbag, look." She gestured with her empty arms. "I've got two small children at home. They'll be asleep by now. Please, don't make them wake up tomorrow and find out their mummy hasn't come home. Just," she paused, weighing up what she was about to say. "Just imagine if it was your mother."

"My mother?" He asked, throwing back his head and laughing. It was a completely joyless sound, like two metal plates being ground against each other. There was no warmth in it at all. "I have no mother." Something seemed to have changed about him. Had his skin always been so pale, paper white in the moonlight? He looked somehow bigger yet thinner, the onesie hanging off his frame. And hadn't the onesie been a cheerful ocean blue, not the dark, threatening navy it was now? "And this isn't about money." Even as he said this, a slight click came from his hand, and the very thing she'd been afraid of jumped from his fingers, catching the light and winking wickedly at her. She glanced very quickly down at it, seeing a short wooden handle and a long silver blade.

Her heart jumped still further. Surely he couldn't really be planning to? Not here, in the middle of the street?

"I'll scream." She whispered, trying desperately to think of something, anything, to keep him back.

"Why? I have done nothing to you. We are just talking on the street on this pleasant summer's evening." He grinned skeletally. "That's all I want to do, Mrs Elizabeth Monica Porter."

She started, unable to keep the surprise from her eyes.

"How do you know-?"

"I know everything about you, Mrs Porter." He took a step forward, looming over her, black fire alight in his eyes, his teeth still bared in his ghastly grimacing grin. She looked up into the face that the cowl covered.

And gasped.

It was impossible. This wasn't real. She'd had too many drinks, she was dreaming, she'd had some sort of nervous breakdown and was hallucinating. It couldn't be real. It just couldn't be.

"Please, don't go anywhere, Mrs Porter." He rasped. "I'm sure you've worked out by now who, or what, I am. So you know it would be very much in your best interests to do exactly as I say."

"Wh-who-why?" She couldn't get the words out.

"Why? Why what?" He was still standing over her, looking down with those burning eye sockets. "Why you? That's what they normally ask. What have they done to deserve a visit from me? I never bother answering that. There's never a good enough answer. So many never deserve it, but that's life, I suppose. Or, it is until I show up." He paused, looking down at his dog, which had sat on the pavement, looking at her intently, as if expecting her to run. "Or maybe you're wondering why I've bothered stopping and talking to you at all, and not just done my job. That would be a smart question to ask, Mrs Porter."

"Wh-why are you a t-t-teenaged boy with a f-f-fluffy dog-g-g?" She managed to get out through her trembling teeth.

The hooded figure threw back his head again and laughed, just as hollowly and humourlessly as before.

"Now that is a new one!" He exclaimed. "So many people find me looking different to how they expect, but they never stop to ask why." He shook his head, the cowl swishing from side to side. "Well, since you have amused me so, I will indulge you." He paused a moment, and then everything changed, and she saw him as he should have been.

Hooded and robed, skeletal white hand emerging from the sleeve, no longer holding a knife but gripping a wooden pole that stood taller than he was. A silver sliver of moonlight arced from the top of the pole, pointing to the ground beneath it. The dog had changed too. It was now up to her chest, fur matte-black and bristly, eyes yellow and glaring. Saliva dripped from the white daggers that curved from between the lips, a low growling in its throat as it watched her, waiting to pounce.

"This is perhaps more like what you would have expected." He whispered, his voice barely audible in the still night air. "But it does make getting to know people so much harder. You see, people tend to turn and run away if they see me like this. Unless it's All Hallow's Eve, of course, but I'm not allowed out then for obvious reasons. But why the boy? With his sci-fi jumpsuit and his braces, his cuddly dog bouncing by his side?" His teeth flashed at her, even without the braces, as he spoke. "Because it amused me. I like seeing how people react to the most non-threatening things. It makes the big reveal so much more fun."

He paused again, and something seemed to change in his posture. His stance became more stooped, his spine arching a little more.

"But you knew something was wrong. When you first saw me. I could tell. You were scared. And that ruins all the fun."

"If you're going to kill me, just do it." She said, surprising both herself and the figure before her. Even the hound's eyes widened a fraction.

"My, my. It seems someone is a little eager." He mused. "No, Mrs Porter. I am not here to kill you. Your time is not now."

"Then why are you here?"

"Why am I here? Isn't it obvious?" He looked down at Barghest. "I'm walking my dog. I may not have a heart, but even I have a heart." He glanced at her, and in that one look she felt him see right through her. "It was so lovely to meet you, Mrs Porter. Although, I hope you'll forgive me for saying I hope we don't meet again soon. And now, I must bid you adieu." With that, he strode past her, the dog's heavy footfalls thumping along the ground. For a moment, she stood, paralysed, unable to believe what had just happened. Then, she turned around, determined to catch one last look at him.

He wasn't there.

Instead, a portly gentleman was striding along the pavement, in full coat tails. A basset hound trotted along at his side, long ears flopping almost to the ground, long snout skimming the tarmac as it followed a scent. In his other hand, he carried a long wooden walking cane with a silver handle, the metal tip rapping against the pavement. The man had a fine black top hat on his head, and the wire of a monocle curling down from his left eye. There was a thin, neatly trimmed white beard on his chin, and curly silver hair just showing beneath the top hat. He appeared in the glow of one streetlight, and then disappeared into the darkness beyond.

She almost laughed. The appearance he had adopted was distinctly comical, not threatening at all to anyone. Then, the laugh died in her throat as she realised.

That was exactly the point.

"I may not have a heart, but even I have a heart." I really like that line. I know it's somewhat egocentric to quote myself, but I just love the idea of the Grim Reaper, of Death himself, having feelings and emotions, just like us humans. A lot of stories have been told about people meeting Death and Death being a lot like us, but I think I am

the first to write a story about Death taking his Hellhound for a walk. I wanted to write a more positive representation of a figure who is so often (literally) demonised, to show that just because someone has a fearsome and threatening appearance, it doesn't mean they can't be gentle and caring underneath.

Patient 0039

Report: Patient 0038

Name: Samantha Louise Bailey

Date of Birth: 21/06/2002

Weight: 65kg

Height: 158cm

Hair Colour: Fair

Eye Colour: Brown

Admitted: 21:43 07/02/2028

Reason(s) for Admission: Wounds on stomach and neck. Possible bites. Heavy bleeding and shock.

Treatment Administered: Stitches applied, anti-infection drugs administered. Admitted to Hutton Ward at 22:29.

Attending Doctor: Martin Chaplain

Other Notes:

> 22:29: The ward is now reaching capacity. We will possibly need to expand into the neighbouring Alexandra Ward if more patients are admitted.

> 00:21: Patient has a fever and chest pains. Painkillers and fluids have been administered. This bares all too striking a resemblance to the previous cases.

The report, like all of them, is brief, and I shake my head. I can access the latest news from the hospitals as soon as it is placed in their systems, but none of it is of any help to me. Anyone who looks like they might be of interest to us is automatically sent to me, but only a few have actually been relevant. Even then, they're not helpful. I need new symptoms, not just more of the old ones. I want developments, not repeats.

There are a series of photographs attached to the file, showing the injuries that Patient 0038 bares. I find it easier if I think of them as just numbers, not people. Stops me getting emotionally involved, keeps me focused on my work.

Well, at least it did.

The first photo shows an attractive young woman stretched out on a bed, an oxygen mask strapped to her face, an IV cannula feeding into the back of her hand. She is pale skinned, very slender, her blonde hair spread on the pillow. The wounds are clear enough, startling red against the white skin. Two ragged holes, one just below her ribcage, the other on the side of her neck, gape like hideous mouths. Patient 0038 got lucky. If the wound on her neck had been a little further round, it would have been her jugular. She wouldn't have made it to the hospital.

I take off my glasses and rub my eyes. I don't have to glance at the mirror that sits beside my computer to know they are bloodshot. It's been at least two weeks since I got a proper night's sleep, only grabbing brief naps here and there as my work allows. I know that I can't work to my absolute utmost if I'm not well rested, but time is of the essence here. I can't afford to miss an important development because I'm taking a catnap.

The room is cluttered, papers scattered around the computer monitor, boxes of files stacked up beside my chair, the draws of the filing cabinet open and rifled through. A foldout camp bed is shoved against one wall, the surface just as strewn with reports and references. The desktop of the computer is similarly busy, document upon document competing with page after page of research filled browser pages. I have to move a pile of cardboard containers just to turn and make my way out of the office and into the lab, which is as gleaming and empty as the office is grimy and crowded. Fresh samples had just arrived from Patient 0021 when the report of Patient 0038 came in. No useful information there.

I open the first test tube, insert the pipette, and draw out a small volume of the dark liquid. A drop falls onto the slide, the glass cover is dropped on, and the slide, very carefully, lifted onto the microscope. I remove my glasses a second time, and press my eye against the lens. A red-brown blur greets me. The microscope is unfocused, still set to the last sample I had. Skin cells are so much larger than blood cells. I rotate the lens carrousel to the highest magnification, and lower the stage until I can see the tiny discs. Just as before, the double dips on the cells have filled out, destroying the bi-concave shape. That's what caused the deepening in the red colour; less oxygen is being carried by the cells. This explains the reduction in fine motor skills the other patients have displayed. I make a brief note on the pad beside the microscope.

Ask for nerve sample from patient

If this thing is attacking the red blood cells, it could reach the nervous system too. That could explain some of the symptoms we've been seeing. Maybe we'll find some answers there.

The next test tube contains a colourless, transparent liquid, not very much of it, the viscosity making it difficult to draw into the pipette. When I put it under the 'scope, I see much what I expected: high levels of the pathogen cells clearly visible. We still have to term it a pathogen, because we don't actually know what it is yet. It's shown a viral immunity to antibiotics, a parasitic ability to transfer itself and the reproductivity of bacteria. We have no real clue what it is, or where it came from.

Some people think it's one of these new superbugs you always hear them scaremongering about on the news, the ones that will surely spell humanity's doom. MRSA and all that. No. This isn't MRSA.

It's so much worse.

Other people think it came from animals, something that someone caught while doing something they shouldn't with a monkey or something. They're wrong too. This thing isn't natural.

This thing was made in a lab. That much is clear enough to me. And it was made to do one thing.

Kill.

I turn back around to the fume cupboard at the back of the lab, where I've got samples of the pathogen in various solutions of chemicals. So far, none of them have come close to touching it. This thing has an incredible resistance to acids, alkalis, it can survive sub-zero temperatures and raging heat. Nothing we've done has stopped it reproducing, and all of the rats we've tried test cures on on have ended the same way.

Even so, I go to the freezer next to the fume cupboard and take out the petri dish anyway. No harm in checking. But a quick examination is all I need to see that the cold hasn't stopped them one bit. They're still alive, and they're still spreading.

We're doing our best to keep things very hushed up. We don't want people to panic. So far, our luck has held. People haven't yet connected the incidents, haven't yet worked out that they're all related. Soon, though, some investigative journalist, or some nosy cop, will work it out. They always do. As soon as that happens, we're going to be in the full media spotlight. Everyone will be looking to us for answers, for explanations, for cures. For hope.

They're going to be bitterly disappointed.

All of the experiments are unchanged from when I left them. None have displayed a dramatic colour change or a sudden plume of fumes that would signal some sort of reaction, some breakthrough that could help us stop this thing. I shake my head. Nothing we've tried is working. There's been talks of jumping straight from rats to human experimentation, but I won't do that. Not until there's no other option. There are other things to be done before then, though I do not agree with all of them either. Experimental compounds derived from half understood plants combined with synthesised solvents fresh out of another laboratory. Next we'll be doing an Edward Jenner and injecting the patients with other diseases to try and kill this thing.

If it can be killed.

We don't even have a name for it yet. That's one of the scariest things about it. Doubtless the newspapers will come up with their own name for it to fill headlines. They're good at that. Here, we just refer to it as 'The Infection'. What else can we call it?

Thinking about it, the Edward Jenner idea might not be so bad a thought after all. Not straight to injecting our patients with smallpox or anything like that, good Lord no. But in lab conditions, where we can control it...

I scribble another note on the pad on the bench.

Possibility of combining pathogens a la Edward Jenner. In lab conditions could reveal something...

There's no guarantee it will work, but at least it's something new, something that we haven't already tried. Who knows? Maybe it'll surprise us.

There's a knock at the door, and I turn to see a dark haired, very masculine woman in a lab coat standing behind the reinforced glass. Unlike mine, Dr. Jenkins' coat is pristine white, freshly laundered and pressed. Her face is stern and determined, the thin lips tight and unsmiling. I stand, wincing a little, and cross the room to the door. There's an electronic numerical keypad built into the wall next to it, and Jenkins and I punch the codes in at the same time. There's a buzz as the magnetic seal is disengaged, and the door slides aside.

"Charlotte. Come in." I say, turning and walking back to my chair, trying to hide the pain each step causes me. I collapse into the seat, looking at the other doctor, who's stood beside the bench with the microscope. The security door quietly closes behind her, resealing itself.

"Anything new, Robert?" She asks in her clipped, staccato voice. I shake my head.

"Same stuff, Charlotte." I gesture at the microscope. "Degrading of the biconcave shape of the red blood cells, and dozens of the little blighters swarming around in the saliva. No new reactions with the chemicals or to the temperatures." I sigh. "I really don't know what we can do. This thing is incredible. Every time we try and analyse it genetically, it mutates into something different so we're back to square one. It's like it was designed to avoid being cured. I still think-"

"For God's sake Robert." Dr Jenkins snaps at me. "We can't say that this thing is some sort of biological weapon. As soon as we start talking about that, someone will let it slip to the news and then we'll be up to our necks in it. We can't even entertain the possibility."

"But come on, Charlotte. Surely you can see."

"What I can see doesn't matter, Robert. You know our instructions. We've got to keep this as quiet as possible. We throw that term around, someone will hear about it. We can't let that happen."

I shake my head.

"I need a nerve sample from Patient 0028," I say. "I want to see if this thing attacks the central nervous system as well."

"Patient 0028 is dead." Jenkins says in a heavy voice. "They died half an hour ago."

"Natural causes?" I ask with morbid hope. Jenkins shakes her head sadly. "The same as the others?"

"Afraid so."

"Anyone else infected?"

"Not that we know. Travis, one of the guards, was attacked, but he seems unhurt. We're putting him into confinement for twenty-four hours to be on the safe side, but he should be ok."

"That's good to hear." I hesitate a moment. "I had the idea that we try combining this thing with other pathogens here in lab. You know, sort of like Jenner."

"Jenner? You mean Edward Jenner? The smallpox guy?"

"Yeah. I don't know if it'll do anything, but it's gotta be worth a shot, right?"

"That's awful risky, Robert. We've seen what this thing does to a human host. If we put it in a pathogenic host, who knows what it'll do?"

"That's why I'm saying we do it here. Off the books. I'll do it myself. Come on Charlotte, this could be what we need." She pauses a moment, thinking.

"Ok. I'll see what I can do. We don't have many pathogens here at base, but I should be able to get you streptococcus, norovirus, maybe mumps if there is any. Just be careful Robert. Don't go Frankensteining anything dangerous." I smile and shake my head at her.

"I'll be ok Charlotte. Hold a moment." I take the pad, scribble down a couple more pathogens on the page, tear it off, and hand it to her. "See if you can get us samples of some of these. I want to try working with them." I turn back to my seat. As I do so, my leg buckles under me, almost sending sprawling to the highly polished lab floor. I catch myself on the edge of the bench to steady myself, wincing.

"You ok Robert?" Jenkins asks, a rare note of concern in her voice.

"I'm fine." I try to force a laugh as I turn back to her. "I'm just weak at the thought of having so many lovely diseases to play with." Jenkins doesn't laugh back. She's watching me closely.

"You sure you're alright?" She says again. "You're pale, like corpse white, and you're sweating buckets." I was hoping she wouldn't notice the rivulets of water I could feel running down over my forehead.

"I said I'm fine. Just a little hot in here. And I haven't slept properly in days."

"Maybe you should take a short break?"

"Don't be stupid. I've got work to do." I take a breath in. "I'm sorry. I didn't mean to snap like that. Maybe you're right. Maybe I should take a little rest. What time is it?" Jenkins glances at her watch.

"Its one oh five in the morning."

"I'll have a rest at two. I just want to sort a few things out."

"Alright. You look after yourself Robert. I'll have the samples sent to you as soon as I can."

"Thanks Charlotte."

Just as she reaches the door, she turns back.

"Did you see the news report? The one about the man found dead?"

"No?"

"Police found a body this evening. Head smashed in against a wall in a back alley a few blocks from here." She pauses. "Apparently, the victim had wounds to his back and legs that looked like bites. I've had a look at the reports and, well, I think he could have been another Patient if we'd found him."

"You think so?"

"He's got all the signs. Unnatural paleness, darkened blood, excessive saliva production. Of course, we can't tell what he was like when he was alive, but my guess is he was acting unusually aggressive and had very little co-ordination."

"Can we get a hold of the body?"

"The police aren't likely to let us look at it unless we give them a good reason, and we can't give them one yet. But it means there's more of them out there Robert, and they're close. Be careful if you go out, you hear?" I smile, or try to. My face feels rigid.

"Always, Charlotte. Goodnight." She keys in the code, and leaves.

I'm on my feet in as soon as she's gone, grunting, trying to ignore the pain in my leg as I hobble into my office. Surely it can't be the same guy? Not the one I ran into? He can't be. He was just some crackhead looking for cash that I'd knocked out in that alley. I didn't kill anyone, and he definitely wasn't a potential Patient.

Except, of course, he was.

I'm lying to myself if I try to pretend otherwise.

It was stupid of me to go out. I just wanted a sandwich, a proper sandwich, not the slimy ham between two pieces of soggy cardboard bread they give us here. He'd just jumped at me out of the blue as I was going down the alley, between the end of a row of terraced houses and the supermarket. It had all happened so fast. A blur of movement, a flash of blinding pain in my leg, a terrible, terrible grunting. In desperation, I'd grabbed the back of his head, yanked him off my leg, and slammed it against the alley wall. And, despite what the films will have you believe about the strength of nerds, I can put quite a lot of force behind my blows.

Back in the office, I drop my trousers, examining the bloody bandage I'd hastily wrapped around the bite in my leg. It is thoroughly stained, more red than white on the thin material. The skin around it is a tight, shiny white, the wound itself an angry red. Red streaks are creeping up and down my leg around it.

I turn back to the computer, open the recording program, hit begin, and record what will surely be my final intelligible words on this earth.

"Eighth of February 2028, one oh seven am. My name is Robert Gladstone. I have been infected with the carnem mors virus. If I were to live, I would be Patient 0039. But I am not going to live." At least I have name for it now. "I was infected this morning at roughly nine am, showing a relatively short incubation period. I leave all my research on this computer and in the files around it. To whichever of my team finds this, do not stop. Find a cure. It is too late for me. But not for the planet."

I shut off the computer, feeling the heat rising inside me. And the hunger. I've never been so hungry.

It's funny. All the books, films, TV shows, even video games. You'd think we'd be prepared for this sort of thing.

But how exactly do you prepare the day that humans turn into flesh eating monsters?

I lean back in the chair. The door out of the lab is locked, so there's no risk of me running out and biting anyone. When they come, they'll be able to deal with me.

It's at this point in the films that I'd pull out a gun or something, kill myself before I turn. But I have no gun. All I can do is sit here, waiting for death.

Yeah, it's zombies, if you didn't get it. But I didn't want to just write the classic, blood-soaked, high-action zombie story that looks good on TV. I wanted to roll things back to the beginning, when things are just kicking off. So I decided to do a scientist, in his lab, trying to find a cure. Not just for the world, but for himself. I've always been interested in the ideas of characters being aware of their own mortality, of a clock ticking down. After all, death comes for all of us. Other than taxes, it's the only certainty in life.

When Worlds Collide

The light in the distance was small. Very small, and flickering, like a candle caught in a breeze. Every few seconds it would disappear, the darkness of the forest becoming total once again, until it bravely burst back into life. It could be a small bonfire, or it could be a Mganga's flame. Either way, it didn't matter. What it meant was people.

The girl pulled a wire, and the metal beast she was sat astride began its lumbering walk through the trees. Small shrubs and branches were flattened under its immense titanium feet as it crunched its way through the leaf litter. She winced. The chumarhin, as the natives called them, were not exactly suited for stealthy movement. The huge metal rhinoceroses were every bit as big and heavy as their flesh and blood counterparts, and all the louder for the pistons and gears that it had for joints and muscles. A more agile machine, perhaps a chumandege, would have been quieter, and faster too. While they might have lost the ability to fly, the long, ostrich-like legs and much lower bodyweight made them so extremely valuable. Hardly surprising that the Pluto Corps had begun capturing them for use as battle mounts.

Still, they had to learn to reprogram the flightless chromium birds first. They hadn't known what they were losing by casting her out.

The chumarhin groaned, its metal plates complaining at the long journey. Its joints were knackered and its power source was failing. She'd been lucky to find it, though, on the way to the scrapheap as it was. Without it, she never would have been able to make the journey. She put a hand to her side, feeling the slickness soaking through the thin bandage and two layers of clothing. During the journey she hadn't dared stop to examine it beyond binding it with the linen strips, but she could tell that she was going to be in serious trouble if she didn't get it looked at soon. If it was a Mganga that had cast that fire in the distance, maybe they could heal it for her.

If they didn't kill her first.

Sparks flashed from an open access panel by her left calf. In their brief glow, she could make out the device she'd inserted into one of the ports. It still seemed to be in working order, and, at least so far, her mount hadn't thrown her off. The light was closer now, and she could see that it did indeed seem to be magical in nature. It had a strange whiteness to it that whispered of sorcery, the flames hanging in a sphere about two feet off the ground. That meant the Mganga that had cast it had to be nearby. The question was, where were they?

She got her answer when she was only about ten feet from the little ball of fire. Suddenly, she heard two sharp hisses, and a crackling of blue sparks burst from the head of the chumarhin. The metal beast groaned one last time, then crumpled forwards, its thick legs folding beneath it as is fell to the forest floor. The access panel sparked a few last times, as if in one last act of life. Then, it was gone.

The girl hadn't seen where the shots had come from, but she had no doubt what they were. Electrically charged arrows, crudely fashioned from metal tipped shafts with tiny batteries attached to them. She'd studied the Wenyeji enough to know that, over the centuries, they'd developed weapons and techniques to defend themselves from the beasts, both machine and magical, that roamed their lands. Not that that had done them much good when the visitors from heaven had come down.

Very slowly, she disembarked from the metallic corpse, hands held high for the benefit of the people who she knew would be watching her from the darkness of the trees. She knew they could see the pistol strapped to her thigh, but they would surely see she wouldn't be able to draw it and fire without receiving an arrow in the chest. Exhaustion was weighing her down like lead blocks, and it was all she could do to stay standing. She wasn't a threat.

Not that they would hesitate to kill her anyway.

"I am not your enemy," she called out to the darkness. Sadly, her post hadn't required her to learn the native language; she just had to hope there was someone there who could understand. "I've been hurt. I need help."

Very slowly, doing her best to appear non-threatening, she lowered her hands, unbuttoned her jacket and lifted up the t-shirt beneath. Doing so made her grimace in pain. They wouldn't be able to see the wound through the bandage, but hopefully the sight of the soaked dressing, and the blood she could feel seeping out around it, would convince them help her.

"Please," she said again. "Does anyone here understand me?"

There was no answer.

Then, a figure stepped forward, melting out of the shadows like a wraith. Maybe he'd learned some sort of concealment charm, or he'd adapted some camouflage tech he'd salvaged from a machine.

He spat something at her in a harsh, guttural voice. She didn't move. She was too scared. The man towered over her, at least six and a half feet tall, his bare arms thick with hard muscle. He wore a mix of fur, fabric and metal, overlapping plates acting as armour on his chest and shoulders, thick pelt stitched together on his legs. He had a cape and cowl fashioned from what looked like wolf skin, the jaw jutting out over his forehead. The jaw had to be a foot and a half long. She'd heard the beasts here were bigger than the ones back on Earth, but she'd never expected to see something like this. She was just glad she hadn't met the wolf while it was alive.

He barked at her again, anger rising in his voice. He was holding a spear in his right hand, five feet of black wood, the head another six inches of gleaming steel. From the way he was holding it, he could either hurl it, with pinpoint accuracy, she had no doubt, or lunge forward and skewer her. Either way, if she moved, she would die. A rifle was strapped across his back, one of the standard issue ones she herself had seen many times at base.

Her head was swimming. The trees were closing in on her like a crowd of strangers, the trunks encircling her. She tried to breathe, but it caught in her throat. The forest was spinning and blurring around her, the trees melting into each other. There was a pounding in her ears that she vaguely knew was her own heart, but it didn't sound human. It was beating at least twice a second, the heart of a caged animal knowing it is about to be slaughtered.

"Please..." She whispered. Then, the world twisted around her, and she fell forward into empty space.

*

Figures drifted in and out of her consciousness, passing like ghosts through her mind. She was being carried through the forest, unseen hands holding her. Where was she going?

Voices, indistinct, saying things she didn't understand. It sounded like an argument, but she was only vaguely aware of it. The hands were still supporting her, but she could barely feel them. She couldn't even tell if she was upright or not.

She was on a bed, soft furs tickling the back of her neck. How had she got there? Where was she? She tried to speak, but the words wouldn't come, her throat too dry and constricted. Pain like fire was blazing through her side, more intense than anything she had ever experienced.

A figure. Looming out of the semi-darkness. Her vision was blurred, out of focus. Her heart raced as terror gripped her; something wasn't right. The head was too long, too tall, strange, branch-like growths protruding from it. Was this some kind of demon, some ancient spirit that had arisen to kill her? She wanted to get up, but her limbs seemed to be made of lead, liquid metal filling her veins instead of blood. She tried to scream, but only the tiniest of squeaks escaped her lips. The shape moved back out of her field of view, and her eyes closed again.

A delicious smell, thick and mouth-watering, reached her nostrils. Her stomach growled, an angry beast that demanded sustenance. The rim of some sort of bowl was pressed against her lips, but some instinct kept them tightly sealed.

A voice, a beautiful, soft voice, spoke from the darkness.

"Drink. It is soup. You are need the food."

It was speaking in English. Broken English, but English nonetheless.

She couldn't keep her lips closed any longer. She parted them, and felt the soup pour into her mouth. It was incredible, gamey and rich, a creamy thickness to it that spread the taste through her mouth. As she swallowed, she could feel it travel down to her stomach, warming her entire body from the inside out. The warmth seemed to quell the fire in her side, replacing the pain with a sense of peace. She kept drinking, swallowing as fast as she could, desperate to take in as much as she could before it could be taken away.

"You are hurt bad," The voice continued. It was soft but deep, a voice that promised comfort and safety. "I am try to heal you. It be very painful." She tried to answer again, but could muster no words. "Do not you talk," the voice soothed. "You sleep. It is less painful." Her eyes closed again, the taste of the soup still on her lips, the warmth still spreading through her body.

When she next awoke, she was instantly aware of two things: the pain in her side was gone, and she was naked. She was lying on a soft mattress, filled with what felt like hay or long grass of some kind, soft furs laid over the top. She was covered by some sort of patchwork quilt of pelts, the different coats stitched together with infinite care. The furs felt soft and comforting against her bare skin.

The bed was in some kind of tent, a big one, the material stretched tight over rigid metal poles. Her bed was in the centre of the structure, just below the central pillar. This pole must have been ten metres tall, reaching up to the fabric ceiling high above. From the light spilling in through the flap that served as a door, she guessed it was mid-afternoon. Turning her head, she could see other beds set up around her. She was in some kind of rudimentary hospital.

And it was full.

She hadn't noticed it before, but now she started hearing the groans from the other patients. There must have been a dozen men and women lying around her. The air smelled of blood and chemicals.

She sat up in bed, pulling the quilt up over her chest. As she did so, she realised that the bandage around her abdomen had gone. She glanced down, and shrieked.

She was on fire.

There was a small blue flame, blue as the sky, burning on her skin, just where she had torn a ragged hole in herself. There was no pain, no burning, but she instinctively tried to bat it out, slapping her hand against her side. It did nothing to the flame, which barely flickered as her fingers passed harmlessly through it.

"You are awake." The voice came from behind her. The same deep, comforting voice that had spoken to her before.

A man stepped round the edge of the bed into the light. He was dressed in furs, the paws of some kind of huge bear draped over his shoulders to hang over his chest. A large helmet or hat of some kind rose up over his head, antlers twisting like branches outwards. His exposed chest and arms were tattooed with strange symbols and characters, the shapes tracing paths across the dark skin of his pectorals and biceps. She realised she was staring and quickly looked back up at his face.

Two eyes, black as space, peered out at her from beneath the headwear. A prominent, chiselled nose, a square jaw and a thin mouth, the two lips almost disappearing into the skin that surrounded them. Glancing back down again, she saw he had on a belt, lined with tubes and vials and pouches. That at least told her one thing about him: he was a Mganga.

"Please," he said, seeing her looking back towards the flame burning on her side. "Do not you be afraid. It is heal you." He muttered a few words under his breath that she couldn't understand. For a moment, it looked like some of the runes on his skin glowed, very briefly. But then she looked again, and they were as dark and lifeless as they had been before. Looking back at her side, she saw the flame had blinked out of existence.

"Where is my uniform?" There were a hundred questions burning through her mind, but this was the one that came out first.

"Your what?" The man looked confused.

"My uniform. My clothes."

"Oh. I have them. I am bring them." He turned and hurried over to a bench by the other wall. He returned, carrying her camouflage trousers, jacket, undershirt, underwear and boots with him.

"Who undressed me?" She demanded, uncomfortable at the thought that this man could have removed her clothes while she was unconscious.

"Mularea. She is the other Mganga. She helps me." The man also looked embarrassed. "Do not you worry. I do not see anything." The man turned around. "You can put on your... yoonefom?" He said over his shoulder. "I do not watch."

Quickly, she redressed in her uniform, deciding to leave the jacket at the last minute. There was no need for concealment here, and she didn't want to look like the soldiers the Wenyeji were fighting against. She also took the opportunity to check her wound. It was nearly entirely gone, only a fresh scar and the ghost of pain showing there had ever been any injury at all. She wondered briefly how long she had been unconscious.

"What is your name?" She asked when she'd dressed, sitting up on the edge of the bed.

"I am Genéser." The man turned around. "I am the chief Mganga for the village."

"Where did you learn English?"

"When you come down from heaven, I am sent to see you. I stay with you a time, I learn your talk so we can work together." He paused, and a flicker of sadness danced across his face. "But you turn on us. You kill us. So we fight back."

A groan from the other side of the tent drew his attention, and he hurried over to one of the beds, muttering something under his breath as he reached the bedside. A ball of the same blue fire she had seen on her own skin bloomed like a flower between his fingers, drifting down to the dark form lying on the bed.

Suddenly, the door flaps were pulled back, and the man who'd held her at spearpoint in the forest strode in, brows low as storm clouds, eyes burning with anger. The weapon was still present, strapped across his back. He marched right up to her, followed by three other men, and yanked her roughly to her feet.

"Hey!" She protested, pulling her arm from his grip. "What the hell are you doing?"

Genéser rushed back over to her, alarmed at the disturbance, talking quickly in his own language. The spearman barked something back at him, the hatred in his voice barely controlled. She was pulled roughly towards the door, Genéser following close behind, still shouting and gesticulating.

"Genéser?" She called back. "What's happening?"

"You are take for trial." The Mganga was by her side, keeping pace with her as she was marched out of the tent and into the village.

"For what?"

"When you are asleep, your people they come. They follow your tracks and they attack us. We lose many people. Beverder," he gestured at the man with the spear, "he loses his brother. He blames you."

The tracks.

Of course. The chumarhin flattened any and all vegetation in its path, making a track that a child could have followed right to this village. She felt ashamed. Her own selfish needs had brought death and destruction to this community.

But then, above the shame, rose anger. It hadn't been selfishness that had brought her here, it had been desperation. She'd been badly hurt, on the edge of passing out and dying in the forest. She hadn't meant to lead harm to them, so why was she to be tried like she was a criminal?

The village passed by as the party made their way through it. The structures were a strange mix of old and new, gleaming metal pillars holding up battered wooden walls. Exposed circuitry could be seen underneath dry grass roofing, solar panels standing in a row next to a smoking forge. Faces watched her from windows and doorways, women with children huddled at their feet, men with hard set faces and glaring eyes. The smell of blood hung in the air, and there were blast marks on the walls of the houses. Several had been destroyed completely. There had been fighting here, and the village had taken a beating.

Her captors led her along a path that twisted through the village and then out of it, climbing a steep hill with two peaks. A gate in a ten-feet-high wire fence took them out of the village. The fence looked harmless enough, but she saw the wires twisting down to a generator at the gate post, heard the faint warning buzzing. The fence was electrified, a first line of defence against anything, flesh or metal, that would try and enter the village.

Smoke was rising from the top of the lower peak, curling upwards from the summit in a thick grey cloud. As they ascended the hill, a smell caught her nose, a smell she vaguely recognised. It was a meaty smell, like pork being roasted, but much stronger. Her stomach growled faintly again. She didn't know how long it had been since she'd eaten that wonderful soup, but it had to have been a while.

"Genéser?" She whispered. "How long was I asleep?"

"You sleep for two days." The Mganga replied. "The attackers they come yesterday."

The leader of the procession, Beverder, snapped something at Genéser, and he fell silent. She could almost feel the raw anger radiating off the man. Given half a chance, he would stick her like a pig with his spear and leave her to die on this hillside. Of that, she had no doubt.

They crested the top of the hill and, as she took in the scene at the summit, she felt her stomach convulse and she nearly vomited.

The structure at the top of the hill was a cross between some sort of amphitheatre and a courtroom, built into the side of the higher peak. There were rows of seating cut into stone in a rough semi-circle around an open courtyard area, the dirt floor covered with a thin layer of sand. The arena space was about fifty feet across, the seating rising up another ten feet around it. A little way beyond the edge of the amphitheatre, she could make out another building, this one much grander than those she'd seen in the village. It looked old, very old, constructed from wood and stone, the slanting roof two giant slabs of what looked like marble that must have weighed three tonnes each.

In the centre of the seating, a row of elderly Wenyeji sat on a bench, watching the group as they came over the ridge. There were seven of them, three men and four women, each with a grandiose headpiece toping from their heads. The man furthest from her had a leathery crocodile skin cape, the top jaw of the creature, at least three feet long and a foot wide, protruding out over his eyes like the peak of some grotesque cap, hiding much of his face. When it was alive, the animal would have been over twelve feet long. The woman next to him was smaller, more shrivelled looking, her face lined with wrinkles, long grey hair cascading out from underneath the lynx pelt she was using as a shawl. The empty, dead eyes of the creature peered out from the crown of her head, its ears still sticking up, as if listening for some threat. Beside the lynx, a plume of eagle feathers, each one ten inches long, surrounded the face of the third man, his eyes narrow and glaring as the group drew closer.

The three nearest the group were adorned with four-foot twisting antlers, a fiercely tusked wild boar's head and a lion's coat, the thick mane almost concealing the face of the woman wearing it. But it was the central woman whose headpiece was truly breath-taking. An intricately woven owl's nest, beset with jewels amongst the wooden fibres, each gem flashing in turn in the flickering firelight. The huge stuffed owl, its two-foot-long wings spread wide as if in flight, stood in the centre. The owl's eyes were open, the wide orange orbs glaring at her as she was brought before the people who would be her judges, her jury, and her executioners.

In the centre of the arena, a huge fire was blazing. The pyre stood about ten feet tall, built around a metal pillar that could just be seen jutting out of the top amongst the orange tongues. The flames leapt and crackled in the afternoon sunlight, sparks dancing in the rising smoke, the grey cloud twisting up to the blue sky. The breeze drifting over the fire carried the smell of roasting meat to her nostrils, almost making her retch.

Because they were burning bodies.

Even as she watched, the last few were tipped off a cart onto the fire, the flames licking hungrily at them as they took hold, devouring the corpses. They wore the uniform of the Pluto Corps., the khaki material stained red in places from arrow, spear, knife and gunshot wounds. She didn't recognise any of the faces she could see, but she still had to turn away in horror, knowing that these were her people who had been killed by the Wenyeji, and it had been her that had led them to their deaths.

The Wenyeji may have lost a lot of fighters, but the soldiers that had attacked them had come off worse.

As she drew closer still, she saw what looked like a door cut into the rock beneath the Elders' bench. It was the most fantastic door she'd ever seen; at least eight feet tall and four feet wide, bigger than any man could ever be.

The woman with the owl headdress stood up, and the procession halted. Before she could say anything, Genéser stepped forward and called out in their language, sounding pleading and almost scared.

He was silenced by a simple raise of the woman's hand.

The mouth beneath the nest opened, the voice loud and clear. She couldn't understand the words, but there was no doubting the authority and power within it. This was the undisputed leader of the tribe, and when she spoke, you listened. The voice radiated out across the hilltop, and for a moment, even the fire seemed to hesitate in its flickering dance.

"The Ajíngu she says I am allow to talk for you." Genéser whispered when the Ajíngu had finished. "You talk. I am talk to them."

She stepped away from the group that had brought her here, shrugging off the hands that held her. Next to her, the fire crackled and popped in anticipation, the flames seeming to glow extra bright.

"My name is Mary Graceback." She said. "I was an engineer and technician for the Pluto Corps." Behind her, she heard Genéser rapidly translating her words to their tongue, hoping that nothing got lost in translation. Mary kept her gaze fixed firmly on the seven people who sat above her. "We came to your world in search of recourses. Our own planet is dying, and we were looking for ways to save it." The Ajíngu raised her hand again, speaking down to Genéser with undisguised contempt.

"She says you lie." He translated. "She says you come here for war, you come with weapons to hunt us."

"No, that's not what happened!" Desperately, Mary tried to think of a way to explain the situation. "We were looking for intelligent life with advanced technology." She said, hurriedly. "We had detected signals from this planet, and seen your metal beasts moving around. We came here hoping to work with you. I was just a mechanic. I fixed things, mended and programmed computers. I never knew what was going on outside the base I was at. We were told you attacked us, that we were only defending ourselves from you." She shook her head. "We were lied to." Genéser, still speaking as fast as he could, nodded at her encouragingly. "I was fixing a computer of a Brigadier when I found a message I wasn't supposed to see. Your planet is like ours. So much like it, that the decision had been made to make this our new home. Our orders had come in to exterminate you. All of you, and take your planet as ours.

"I was caught, and they would have killed me if I hadn't gotten away." She lifted up her undershirt to show the scar on her side. "I did this to myself. When we joined the Corps., we were all injected with a device under the skin. It lets them keep track of us, gets us to certain parts of the base, lets us access certain computer files. I cut it out of me on the way out, but I did a poor job. Its only due to the kindness of your Mgangas that I'm still alive."

Another brief burst from the Ajíngu, quickly translated.

"How do you control the chumarhin you come on?"

"My speciality before I joined the Corps. was software manipulation. Among my other duties, I was part of a development team that was tasked with finding a way to override the machines that live here. Just before I discovered the message, I finished a program that allowed me to hack into the machine's operating system. All I have to do is get up close to the machine and plug in..." She dug around in her pockets, horrified to discover that the device wasn't there. Of course. She'd left it in the metal corpse of her ride. "It's a device I created. It gives me control over the machines. I left it in the one that brought me here; if you let me go and get it, I can show you." Mary waited while Genéser finished communicating her words to the Elders. A quick and heated discussion, one of the men standing up in outrage and protest, flashed across the bench, before the Ajíngu stood once more. Her face was solemn and cold. When she spoke, her voice carried no emotion.

"They believe your story," Genéser said, a note of sadness in his voice. "But they say you pay must for the lives we lose. We are let Gedina she decide. You are face trial by fight."

"Fight?" Mary said in disbelief. "No, no! I'm not a soldier, I've got no combat skills! Whoever you put me against will tear me apart."

"I am sorry." Genéser looked genuinely upset. "The council are not change they mind. You are fight, or you are die."

"Please!" She begged as she was pushed towards the arena floor. "Genéser! Help me!" But the Mganga just stood there, shaking his head in apology. There was nothing he could do.

Beverder gave her a hard shove from behind, sending her stumbling onto the sand, almost falling flat on her face. As it was, she toppled forward onto her knees, catching herself with her arms just before she bit the grit. She stayed there for a moment, curled in a protective ball on the ground, feeling twelve pairs of eyes watching her. Seven pairs who would decide her fate. Four pairs that hated her for what she had brought to them. And one pair who had been the closest thing to a friend she'd found among the Wenyeji.

The Ajíngu spoke again from her perch on the bench, and Mary noticed that the huge stone doors beneath them had started to grind their way open, sliding sideways on hidden rails within the rockface. At the same time, she realised that metal fences were rising out of the ground around her, trapping her within the arena. Just like the ones that protected the village, these too were electrified. The power cables here were much thicker, almost like long black snakes twisting around the fenceposts and down to the ground.

"Our ancestors they build this place years ago." Genéser said from behind the rising metal barriers. "They use it as a place to test truth. We use it for same thing. Here, the Goddess Gedina she chooses if you live or if you die. Here, you fight chumagunuwe."

The stone doors finished rumbling aside as Mary stood up, a gaping black mouth now yawning before her. She could hear something shuffling its way along the tunnel behind it. It was moving slowly, sluggishly, something big from the sound of it. Then, the shuffling became a trotting, and finally a galloping as whatever it was sensed prey. A thunderous rumbling shook the ground beneath her as the thing she was to fight charged towards her and burst out into the light.

A roaring, gleaming blur exploded onto the sand, kicking up the loose surface in great plumes. The machine stood taller than she was, a swollen barrel-like body on short, thick legs. Its metal hooves pounded across the sand towards her, carrying the metal beast, which must have weighed at least two tonnes, at astonishing speed. Two dark, cold cameras glared at her from its arrow-shaped head. Below them, twin swords, each two feet long and curving wickedly skywards, flashed in the sunlight. The machine was charging straight for Mary, aiming to either impale her with its tusks or crush her beneath its hooves.

Mary reacted instinctively, hurling herself sideways out of the path of the silver locomotive that was bearing down on her. The metal boar (or it might have been a warthog; she never had known the difference) flashed by her like a bullet. She hadn't quite moved in time, and the machine's bulging abdomen caught her a glancing blow to her foot as she dived sideways. The impact wasn't enough to hurt her, but it sent her spinning onto the sand, landing face first in the grit. That was enough to hurt her.

Spitting out grains and rubbing them from her eyes, Mary stumbled to her feet, desperate to keep moving, knowing it was her only chance to stay alive. If she stayed still, she would be trampled into the ground. The chumagunuwe had surprising manoeuvrability for a creature of its size, wheeling around at the far edge of the area to attack her again. Its head was down, its tusks pointed towards her like the horns of a charging bull.

What could she do? She had nothing on her person but the clothes she was wearing, and there was nothing in the arena beyond the sand and the fencing surrounding it. They had provided her with no weapons, no tools, no anything that she could use to defend herself. If this was how they expected their Goddess to show mercy, then it wasn't surprising that they lived in perpetual fear of her.

The chumagunuwe was nearly upon her once more, racing across the sand with malice. Mary waited, then dived away again. But this time, the machine had predicted it. As Mary moved, it flicked its head to one side, its lethal tusk catching her on the outside of her thigh as it screamed past. Mary cried out in pain, falling to the sandy floor. The group of Wenyeji warriors, who'd taken seats in the stands, cheered. Blood was running down her leg, a long wound torn in her combat trousers and across the flesh. It wasn't deep, but it was bleeding heavily and would be seriously debilitating if she didn't get it stitched. If she'd been just a few inches further right, it would have torn open her femoral artery. The sand around her was slowly staining red. Crimson dripped from the boar's tusk as it watched her. She stayed where she was, lying on the floor, too shocked and too scared to stand. She glanced upwards, and saw the seven Elders looking down at her. The Ajíngu had a half smile on her face, as if she was pleased with what she was seeing.

Anger rushed through Mary's body like fire. How dare they sit there and watch her die? How dare they condemn her as a criminal without justification? She was going to show them. She wasn't going to just die on her knees. She was going to beat this chumagunuwe and then she was out of here.

Slowly, painfully, she dragged herself to her feet, most of her weight on her left leg. She limped over to the fence, the warning crackling here much louder than it had been outside the village. The effort was too much for her, and her leg gave way, sending her crashing back into the sand. Her back was to them, but she could almost picture the looks of undisguised pleasure on the faces of the Elders as they watched her, weak and helpless, just waiting to be finished off.

But they couldn't see what she was doing with her hands.

Quickly, only half knowing what she was doing, her strength rapidly draining out of her leg, she pulled at the cables connected to the fence. She'd never tear them apart; each one was almost as thick as her wrist. But there were connection points where the individual thin wires joined to form the thick cables. She found one such point and pulled it apart, the end sparking as it wrenched out of its socket. The fence stopped crackling. The power had gone out.

The chumagunuwe still hadn't made its final charge. Mary didn't know if its artificial intelligence had been programmed to feel emotion, but it certainly seemed to be enjoying itself. Let's see how happy it feels in two minutes time, she thought grimly. She pulled on the cable, ripping it from its bindings to the bottom of the fence. She yanked again, and again, each time pulling more and more free until she had about thirty feet of cable. All the while she was wondering why the boar was staying where it was, and not charging her down. Could it be that it really was a mechanical sadist, enjoying watching her slowly bleed to death? Or was it simpler than that? Did it think the fence was still electrified, and charging her would bring it too close to the fatal barrier? In either case, Mary didn't care. She was just grateful she wasn't either speared or crushed. Yet.

She removed the standard issue belt from her waist, pulling it tight around her upper thigh and forcing the pin through the material to create a new hole. Now she wished she'd brought the jacket with her; it would have made useful padding. Never mind; she could do without.

Mary forced herself to her feet, wobbling uncertainly on her injured leg. In her hand was the thick rubber cord, the heavy metal connecting point hanging towards the ground. She stared at the hulking metal beast in front of her, almost challenging it with her eyes. The beast's hollow, dead cameras showed nothing. To her right, the Elders watched on in silent judgement.

And then, Mary charged.

It was so sudden and unexpected that for a moment even the chumagunuwe was unable to process what was happening. The roles had somehow been reversed; it was its job to charge at the human, not the other way around. Yet her she was, hobbling across the sand with determination, something long and black snaking behind her. The chumagunuwe lowered its head, stamped its hoof once, and charged, its tusks at chest level, ready to impale her as soon as she was close enough.

At the very last moment, when she was close enough to see the lens of the camera rotating to stay focused on her, Mary dived sideways, pulling the cable taught. She was unable to stop herself crying out and pain tore through her leg, the exertion almost too much for her. The charging boar raced past her like a bullet, one of the metal plates on its side actually scratching her on the arm as it passed by. But it hadn't considered the cable. It was torn out of her hands, the rubber tubing ripping the skin as it was wrenched away.

But it had done its job.

A sudden clap of thunder made Mary jump as she forced herself back onto her feet. She hadn't even noticed the thick storm clouds blowing in, but sky was now as grey and churning as the sea. The first drops of rain, light and small, began to break against her skin.

The chumagunuwe was lying on its side in the sand, the electrical power cable wrapped around its front legs. When it had torn the cable from Mary's hands, the weighty electrical connector on the end of the cord had whipped around, tying the chord around the metal stanchions that supported the machine. Better still, the boar's struggling had further entangled itself. It couldn't stand up, its metal legs desperately kicking at the air as it tried to right itself. But the cable wouldn't hold it for long. It would only take a matter of seconds for the chumagunuwe's central processing unit to work out that it could tear through the cable if it directed more power to its legs. Mary had to act now.

As fast as her wounded leg would allow, Mary crossed the sand to the boar even as bigger, heavier drops of water began to patter the ground around her. About two metres of the cable at the end with the connector were lying loose on the sand, the metal socket glinting in the now dying fire. Mary grabbed the cable, looped it over the boar's tusk, and pulled with all her strength. The rubber held, strained, and finally broke, the sharp metal edge sheering through it and the metal strands beneath. There was a momentary flash of sparks from the exposed wiring at the same moment that the first bolt of lightning ripped across the sky, the blast of thunder following a second later. The chumagunuwe began to struggle harder, obviously calculating what Mary was about to do. She could see the panel on its neck, the latch winking at her in the lightning flash. She tore the panel open, exposing the circuitry and wires beneath. The machine was incredibly complex, the electronics inside more intricate than she could have possibly imagined. But it didn't matter. They would still react the same way. Mary raised the cable above her head, like a knight raising his sword before he staked the dragon. Above her, lightning exploded through the sky, catching the chumagunuwe's eye. The blank, empty lens showed no emotion, but Mary could imagine the fear it would have felt if it could.

She brought the cable down as the thunder rolled around the arena, the bare wires connecting with the exposed electronics. The metal boar jerked and spasmed, its pistons and gears grinding and locking as current tore through it. It tore through Mary too, throwing her backwards across the arena and into the sand. For a moment, she blacked out, an empty void swallowing her up as she twitched uncontrollably.

When she came around, the few spectators in the stands were on their feet, shouting and gesturing in obvious anger. Looking over at what had been her opponent, she saw steam from the falling rain curling up from the metallic corpse. If it could ever have been called alive, it was now dead. The seven Elders were sat in silence, a look of outrage plastered on each and every face. Slowly, Mary stood up, looking straight at the bench. The Ajíngu got to her feet also, spitting out words in an angry torrent, the glaring eyes of the owl flashing in the lightning. Mary glanced over at Genéser, who was still behind the fence. She couldn't read the look in his eyes. It might have been pride, or it might have been fear.

"They say you are cheat." He said slowly. "You break the electrics to beat chumagunuwe. You are fail the trial."

"I defeated the machine." Mary shouted back angrily. "You never said how I had to do it."

A pause, as the three-way conversation made its way back.

"Trial is act of Gedina. She decide if you win. She give you strength, not you cheat."

"Gedina must have made me cheat."

When this was translated to the Ajíngu, the look of horror on her face could have curdled milk. She opened her mouth to speak again, but as she did so, another burst of light, the brightest and closest yet, split the sky. The bolt, zigzagging down through the air, struck the metal pole in the centre of the pyre, the flames leaping and darting crazily. The old woman stood, stunned. She looked at the fire, then at Mary, then back at the fire. When she spoke again, her voice was slow and full of shock.

"She say that Gedina she sends a sign." Genéser translated, and he couldn't keep the happiness out of his voice. "You are live."

Mary watched as the four guards who'd brought her there left, disgust on each and every one of their faces. Beverder shot her a look of pure hatred as he exited the arena, and somehow, she knew that this 'sign' was not going to change his opinion of her. She took one last look at the machine that had nearly speared, stamped and shocked her to death. She should be dead. It hadn't been Gedina that had saved her. It had been luck and an electric fence.

*

A few hours later, Mary was lying on another straw mattress in a small hut on the edge of the village. The walls were mud and metal, the roof thatch, but it was warm and surprisingly comfortable. Night was drawing in and life in the village was beginning to wind down. The tribe's hunters had come back, dragging the carcass of a six-foot chicken between the five of them. Shortly after them, the scavengers had returned, each with a bag full of metal and electrical parts they'd salvaged from machines. Genéser, at her behest, had asked them to try and retrieve her device from the chumarhin she'd rode in on, but they'd come back empty handed. Apparently, Gedina had taken the metallic corpse away, as she did all the fallen machines.

The giant chicken had been butchered and served as a stew in the village's central hall, a cavernous wooden building lit by electric lights in the ceiling and heated by a roaring fire at one end. Mary hadn't failed to notice the looks the villagers gave her and Genéser as he'd led her to the serving bench and then to a table in the corner of the hall. They looked at her with suspicion, some with fear. But at least they were no longer the hate-filled glances she'd received earlier.

After the food, Genéser had taken her to this cabin, and healed the wound on her leg with another orb of blue fire. She watched in fascination as the symbols tattooed onto his skin glowed while he muttered his incantations, conjuring the flames out of thin air.

"Genéser?" She'd asked. "What happens now?"

"The Elders are talk now about what they are do. They are decide in morning."

"Will you tell them something for me?"

"Yes?"

"Tell them that in exchange for letting me live, I can show the how to control the machines. I will need parts, but I can build another device; I can remember all the code. I can make them fight for you. They can help you win the fight against the Pluto Corps." Genéser had nodded, excitement lighting up his eyes.

"Yes. Yes, I am tell them. This is help us. Thank you, Mery." He rose. "I am go now. You shout if you are need me?"

Mary settled herself back into the mattress and closed her eyes. The day had worn her out and even with the Mganga's magic healing, she still wasn't fully recovered. Pain still rocked her side every time she moved. What would the morning bring? Comradery, or exile? A second chance, or a death sentence?

Her last thought before the darkness washed over her was how in the world a simple girl from Croydon had managed to end up here.

*

Someone was shaking her shoulder, pulling her back to consciousness. She came unwillingly, trying to claw her way back into the pit of sleep.

"Mery? Mery, you wake up."

"Genéser?" She cracked her eyes open. It was still night, the Mganga lit only by a dancing ball of flames, these ones a pale yellow, hovering above his head. "What's going on?"

"The chumagunuwe…" That was all Mary needed to jolt her into wakefulness. Had the machine somehow rebooted itself? Was it tearing a path of destruction through the already damaged village, flattening and impaling anyone in its path? "It is be take."

"Taken? Taken where? By what?" Mary was on her feet, following Genéser as he led her out of the cabin into the village street. He didn't answer her, walking quickly away towards the hill where she'd been tried. She had to break into a jog to catch up with him. The mud was cold and hard under her boots, their breaths misting in the chill night air. While the days here were warmer than on Earth, the nights were far colder. Their analysts suspected that this was part of the reason for the animals being so much larger than their own creatures. She shivered, pulling her arms around her chest. She didn't know where her jacket was, until Genéser pulled it out of the bag he wore at his waist.

"Here. You are cold. I keep this for you."

She slipped it on gratefully, buttoning it up all the way to the neck.

"Thank you Genéser."

Although it must have been well after midnight, the village was alive with activity. People were hurrying back and forth across the street, children huddled in doorways with wide eyes. Genéser took her through the crowds, taking her hand and pulling her into the mass of people, the ball of fire preceding them. Mary was battered from all sides as she was pulled through the churning sea, trying to duck and weave her way until she realised it would be easier to just let herself be dragged through. The two emerged from the other side and hurried up the hill. There was no more smoke rising from the fire, but the embers were still glowing as they crested the mound. Mary caught a glimpse of a blackened, twisted skeleton lying against the side of the remains of the pyre, and turned away.

Genéser lead her over to a group of people standing where the arena had been. The metal fences had been retracted, so she guessed someone had repaired the electronics she'd damaged. As they got closer, she recognised the disformed T above the head of one of the women, the green leather cloak of one of the men. The seven Elders were there, and they were worried. The Ajíngu turned around as they approached, the flames hovering before them, flickering in the cold breeze, revealing the concern in her eyes. She said something quickly to Genéser, who answered, before turning to Mary.

"They ask what you do to chumagunuwe. Why he is take by other machines?"

"I don't know what's happened." Despite her jacket, Mary was shivering in, her hands tucked into her armpits. "What other machines?"

Genéser translated her response, and another tribesman stepped forward. He was short and squat, a selection of tools and parts hanging from his belt, which was on a level with Mary's mid-thigh. He was holding a torch, electric rather than fire, wires trailing down his arm into one of the pouches sewn onto the front of his tunic. He spoke very quickly, the words tumbling out in a rush, the excitement in the words evident to Mary even if the meaning was not. Genéser listened intently, stopping the man once to slow him down, before relaying his meaning. The man's grey eyes shone with elation, the dome of his head shining just as much in the torch light.

"Werkigé he is a mender. He say he is just finish fix the fence," Genéser said. "He hears a noise and he sees machines connect to chumagunuwe. The machines…" He paused, trying to find the right words. "They are like very big bugs. They drag chumagunuwe away. Werkigé he calls the Elders and they come here." Werkigé nodded, although Mary doubted he'd understood what Genéser had said. The Ajíngu whispered something to him, and the mender hurried away towards the building with the stone roof that Mary had noticed earlier.

Mary stood for a moment, trying to put the pieces together.

"Genéser, how long have your people been hunting the machines?"

"We hunt them for years. Since the time of ancestors, when Gedina comes down to kill the sinners."

"But they've never gone extinct?"

"What is, uh, eggstinked?"

"The machines never die out? Disappear?"

"No." Genéser looked confused. "It is said that Gedina creates the machines, as she has from the Beginning."

"Here's what I'm thinking. They can't reproduce naturally, because they're machines. But they're not dying out, so more have to be coming from somewhere. That means they're being made somewhere. I think if we follow these insect machines, we'll find where the rest of them are coming from." A spark of excitement was dancing in Genéser's eyes as he conversed with the Elders. The woman in the lynx fur cut in in argument, but he raised a hand to silence her and carried on. There was silence for a moment after he finished, as the assembled council considered what he said. The Ajíngu stepped forward, towards Mary, the orange eyes of the owl glowing in the darkness. The old woman, her face a shrivelled and wrinkled prune, reached out, and took Mary's hand. The two women looked into each other's eyes, and in that moment Mary felt something travel through her, from the Ajíngu and back again. All at once, she felt the strength of the woman, the determination, the courage. She could sense the emotions and experiences, the thoughts and feelings, the loves and the losses.

And the fear.

The Ajíngu was afraid.

"Follow them." The voice sounded loud and clear, though the older woman had not opened her mouth. The words instead flashed through her head, soft but strong, steadfast yet sympathetic. "Follow them, and find the secrets we lost to time." Mary started, her eyes widening. The Ajíngu smiled at her, the thin mouth twisting upwards, stretching out the lines of her face. She said something to Genéser, who nodded, then turned back to Mary. The ball of fire hovered above his shoulder like some sort of glowing monkey from an old pirate film.

"She says we follow them." Genéser said, a smile breaking out on his own face. "We go now, we find where they go." As they turned to leave, the Ajíngu called out. Werkigé was hurrying after them, carrying a bundle wrapped in rough brown cloth. "They are for you." Genéser relayed. "They belong once to the Ajíngu. She wants you to have them." Mary took the bundle, set it down on the hard ground and unwrapped it. Resting on the top was a long-sleeved tunic, unlike any she had ever seen. It was pure white, the soft fibres expertly woven together in an intricate mesh, the material soft and pleasant under her fingers. As she lifted it up and it unfolded, she saw that there were metal plates, these also white, embedded within the fabric, so carefully attached that it was as if the fibres themselves simply melded together into the metal. She expected the garment to be weighty and unwieldy, but to her surprise it felt lighter than her combat jacket. The plates were positioned to protect the vulnerable areas, the chest, the stomach, the shoulders and elbows, without compromising movement, that much was certain. Mary couldn't even imagine how many hours it had taken to prepare this one item.

Beneath the tunic lay a beautiful curved bow, already strung, with a quiver full of arrows. The bow was jet black, carved from what looked like a single limb of wood, perhaps ebony. It formed a perfect half-moon, the heads of the arrows lying beside it twinkling like stars in the fire light. Looking closer, Mary gasped as she saw that the wood was inlayed with gold, intricate patterns and shapes elegantly embossed onto the surface. Going closer still, she realised that they were the same symbols and runes that were tattooed all over Genéser's body. The same symbols were carved into the arrowheads, the tiny etchings only just visible in the faint light.

"The bow it is magic." Genéser translated as the Ajíngu spoke. "The arrows they are also. They are fly straight and honest. They are not break, and they are... they will hurt machines." Mary nodded, awestruck by the quality of the craftmanship of the weapons.

Just below the bow lay a leather belt, two curved sheaths fixed to the material. Glimmering silver handles twisted out of the top of these, each inlayed with jewels of purple, red, green and white. Mary picked one up and drew the knife from its holder. It came free easily, sliding smoothly out of the leather binding. The blade shone in the firelight, eight inches of gleaming, curved metal, the same white metal that was so cleverly woven into the tunic. She didn't need to test the edge to know that they were sharper than razors. She carefully slid the weapon back into its sheath, then looked up at the Ajíngu.

"Thank you," She tried to say, but it came out as no more than a whisper. "They're beautiful." The old woman didn't need that translated; the meaning was clear. She smiled at Mary, the wrinkles in her face deepening. A pleasant, hopeful smile that seemed to contain all the good will in the world. Then she turned, and walked back to the rest of the Elders.

*

Two hours later, Mary and Genéser were making their way across a flat, grassy plain about two miles from the village. The grass, tipped white with frost, crunched under their feet as they walked, plumes of white rising as they breathed. The Mganga had donned a thick coat, this one made from what looked like wolf skin, the thick grey fur wrapping around him. His fire still burned, hovering before them as they walked, its faint light showing the path. Mary had put on the tunic that the Ajíngu had given her, the belt around her waist, the bow and quiver slung across her back. She hadn't known how good the light white material would be at keeping out the chill, but she felt comfortably warm, liking the feel of the soft fibres against her skin.

The hard ground wasn't as conducive to following tracks as soft mud would have been, but there were still signs to point the way if the two looked for them. If they'd had a team of the tribe's trackers with them, they doubtless would have made much faster progress. Unfortunately, however, Genéser was a healer, not a hunter, and although Mary's own training had included basic survival techniques, tracking had not been one of the lessons. Even so, they didn't feel they'd done too badly thus far, only losing the tracks a couple of times, always finding them again after a bit of searching.

As they went, Mary asked Genéser questions about his life, his tribe, the machines, the Elders, anything that he could tell her. She soon learned that he was an only child, born the son of the village blacksmith but was never taken with metalworking. Ever since he'd been a child, his passion had been helping things. When he was still only a toddler, he'd found a wolf cub with a broken leg, abandoned by its mother and left to die. Even when it was still a cub it was nearly as big as him, but he hadn't been scared. By then, he'd already been identified as one with a connection to the Goddess, one able to manipulate magic to harm or heal. His knowledge of healing charms had been basic at best, but he'd managed to at least stop the wolf's pain before his parents had pulled him away, terrified for his life. Since then, he'd devoted himself to the study of helping things, of finding new cures and techniques for nursing and healing. It was he who had found a way of manipulating fire to heal wounds, like he had done to Mary's, something that had never been done before in the tribe.

"How do you make the fire not burn them?" She asked.

"I do not know. It is... difficult to say." He paused. "It is like I put my feelings into the fire. I tell it to heal, no to hurt." Mary had noticed how much his English had improved in just the short time he'd spent listening to her speak it. Genéser was clearly a fast learner, quick minded and inquisitive.

"Are there other tribes like the Wenyeji?"

"Yes. But they live far from here. The Wenyeji, we are the bigger tribe in the area. The village it is much biggest than you see. We have..." He struggled for a moment. "How are you say lots and lots of ten?"

"Thousands?"

"Thousands. Ok. We have thousands. The Benwígu, they live many miles that way." He pointed roughly north, away from the direction they were going. "They are more small. They have less thousands."

"Do you all speak the same language?"

"We are speak very like. We learn from carvings we find from they who come before."

"And do you all believe in the same Goddess?"

"Yes. Gedina makes all the people in the world. She ties us all together." He stepped round a large dip in the ground, helping Mary to do the same without slipping. She wondered where he'd learned such gentlemanly behaviour. Somehow, she doubted that politeness and manners were something the Wenyeji considered high priority next to hunting and building. "I may ask you something?"

"Of course."

"Why do you come here? Why do you join the... Plooto Cour?"

"The Pluto Corps? I joined them because I had nowhere else to go." She hesitated, unsure whether to continue. "I was born on Earth; that's the planet we all came from, in a place called London. It was just a normal life for me, I suppose. Well, I'd say it was normal. It was probably quite different to yours." Genéser smiled at her, a comforting, encouraging smile that made her feel safe and protected. "I wasn't good at much," She went on. "Except messing with computers. I loved that. Do you have something that just makes the rest of the world go away? That means you don't worry about anything while you're doing it?"

"Yes." Genéser said, his face completely straight. "I sleep." Mary laughed without meaning to. He hadn't been making a joke, but his misunderstanding of the question was distinctly comical. It reminded her of old films, ones that belonged to her father, made by pairs of actors who made people laugh for a living by doing stupid things.

"Why you laugh?" Genéser asked, looking at her in puzzlement.

"Sorry. Sorry, it's nothing." She composed herself. "I mean, is there something that you enjoy so much that you forget everything else?"

"My healing." He replied, understanding. "When I am doing it, nothing else is important. It is just me, and the patient."

"Exactly! That's what it was like with me and computers. I'd spend hours every day playing around with them, taking them apart, building my own, writing the programs. My bedroom looked like the place where computers went to die." They came to the edge of a forest, the tracks not even hesitating before plunging straight into it. At least the trail of debris would make it easier to follow their targets. Mary sat down to rest for a moment on a fallen tree, the thick trunk snapped near the base.

"Anyway, I left school with not many qualifications. My dad refused to support me, and my mum had died of cancer just after I was born."

"What is cansor?"

"It's a disease. The body's cells mutate and grow out of control. There's no proper cure for it, so it usually kills you. My mum had it in her stomach, and it could have been treated, but they didn't catch it in time. My dad raised me all my life, and he did alright. I never went hungry or cold. But he believed that you had to earn your keep, not have it given to you. In his eyes, I'd squandered my chance at getting a good education, so I'd have to work hard to get by, and he wasn't going to help. So when I heard that the Pluto Corps were looking for young people who were looking for adventure, no qualifications needed, I jumped at it." She took a breath, drawing the frigid air into her lungs. "That was eight years ago. I haven't seen my dad since." Mary felt the tears welling up in her eyes, and tried to blink them away before Genéser could see them. But they caught the pale light from the turquoise moon riding the clouds high above them. It was full tonight, a perfect circle, the light blue strangely beautiful against the deep black velvet that was the sky. When the Pluto Corps had first arrived, there had been many jokes made about blue moons. But tonight, Mary could see the beauty in it, and in the landscape around that was bathed in its light. Around it, a sprinkling of stars, much brighter and closer than those visible from Earth, flickered and danced in the heavens.

"I am sorry." Genéser mumbled, sounding pained. "I did not mean to made you cry."

"It's ok. It's not you." Mary said, forcing herself not to cry. She wiped her eyes with the back of her hand and sniffed.

"I may show you something?"

"Sure." Mary tried to smile. "Impress me."

Genéser raised his hands to his lips, cupping the palms before his mouth. Very faintly, almost too quietly for Mary to hear, he began to hum, a soft, pleasant note that seemed to spread outwards in waves from where he stood. He shifted his hands, and the note changed, deepening and rising in volume. He was playing some kind of tune, shifting his hands very subtly to change the notes. It was a beautiful sound, a gentle melody that filled Mary with an incredible sense of calm and ease. She felt her troubles slowly melt away, replaced with a beautiful feeling of tranquillity. The note drifted on the gentle night breeze, carrying into the forest and beyond.

And then they began to rise.

It started so slowly that she didn't even notice it to begin with. First one, then another, and another, then five, then ten. Soon the air was full of them, dancing in the soft wind, shining like the stars so far above them.

"What are they?" She whispered in wonderment.

"We are call them the Nzi Nzi," Genéser replied, pausing briefly in his song.

Within a minute, the air was thronging with them, tiny lights that pulsed and flickered with life. One drifted past her face, a gentle humming that matched Genéser's tune as it floated lazily past. She was reminded of fireflies on a summer's night, only much, much brighter.

"They're beautiful." Mary said, watching the insects as they hovered around them, listening to the soft humming from both them and her companion. More and more Nzi Nzi were rising out of the undergrowth in the woodland ahead, until the whole forest seemed to be alive with floating stars. High above, the blue moon silently watched, drifting as if on the sea, its audience of stars gathered to watch this beautiful sight.

Mary felt a moment of incredible transcendence, of not being there anymore. She was flying, soaring elegantly and gracefully through space, past planets and suns and galaxies. The stars danced around her, the beautiful melody playing in her ears as she flew further and further, until at last she saw a familiar ball of blue and green, streaked with white. Earth, as it had been in its prime, before humanity had begun to kill it. She turned, and let herself be carried down, through the clouds and into the clear blue. Twisting, she saw the islands, so small next to the continent that neighboured them, floating effortlessly amongst the blue. She dove, faster and faster, down towards them. First she saw fields, then forests, then rivers and roads. Now she was flying above a great city, gleaming, soaring skyscrapers, tightly clustered houses, twisting roads and streets. And running though it all, a great silver crack in the landscape that was the river Thames.

Her feet touched down on the pavement. Mary was standing on a road that she knew, surrounded by houses and cars she recognised.

Ahead of her, a flagstone path wound from the wooden gate through a small garden, the lawn meticulously and expertly cut. She didn't need to step on it to know that the third flagstone was loose, or check to see the flowers arranged behind the low brick wall would be violets, tulips and roses. The path led to a door, a soft blue door, a door which, the last time she'd seen it, she wasn't sure she'd ever see again. As she walked towards it, the door opened, and a man, short, bald and a little chubby, appeared in the space. There was a smile playing on his lips, and his arms opened wide as she drew near. She didn't hesitate to go into them, burying herself in his warmth, letting it envelop her. Mary looked up into her father's eyes, into their warm hazel depths.

But they weren't hazel.

They were black, as black as night, crowned by twisting deer antlers, set in a face that wasn't flabby and soft but chiselled and dark. She felt Genéser's arms pulling her in closer, and she held him tight. Around them, the Nzi Nzi continued to drift through the air, swirling around the embracing pair like dancers round a campfire.

*

As the sun began to peak over the horizon, the apex of its golden rim barely visible, the two travellers left the dark confines of the forest, the faint impressions in the ground guiding them ever onward. With the first light of a new day spilling across the planes, they made their way around a great lake, the deep blue water sparkling in the early morning rays. Ahead of them, a towering grey mountain loomed, the craggy face rising steeply upwards right from the base. Looking up, Mary could make out snow topping the peak, its whiteness merging with the white of the clouds around it. The tracks were heading towards it, curving around the lake and continuing dead straight towards the mountain.

Genéser saw her looking at it, and nodded.

"We are call it Muncha Gukiti," he said, pointing to the rocky mound. Following his finger, Mary could see that part of the mountain looked like it had been cut away. A vertical wall straight down from the peak to about a third of the way down, a perpendicular horizontal shelf marking the end of the drop. It was as if someone had taken a photograph of the mountain, cut it into quarters, and then taken away one of the top sections. "That is mean "The Chair of the Goddess". We believe it is where Gedina she comes down to make all life." The name made sense to Mary; the horizontal plateau and the wall behind it did indeed resemble the seat of a chair.

"Has anyone ever climbed it?"

"Not from the Wenyeji, no. The other tribes, maybe they had someone who they climbed it. But we had never heard them said so."

"We're going to have to climb it, aren't we?" She asked, her voice heavy.

"I think so." Genéser replied. "The tracks are go to it."

Together, they crossed the plain towards the grey spire, the tracks clearer in the soft mud around the lake. The ground under their feet began to rise, banking upwards so sharply as they reached it that within minutes their journey had gone from walk to climb, Mary's combat boots sliding over loose shingle as she scrambled upwards. The tracks they were following disappeared as soon as they transitioned from soil to stone, but it didn't matter. A clear path had been etched up the mountain, a route used so many time that rocks had been worn down and the scree disturbed, the loose stones pushed aside. It was clear that something used this path a lot and, by the look of it, was usually dragging something big with it. Mary began to feel more and more uneasy as they scaled the side of the cliff, following the trail. Something didn't feel right.

She tried to take her mind off it.

"Genéser?"

"Yes?"

"Back at the village, when the Ajíngu held my hand, I felt something. It was like she passed something to me. I could feel what she was feeling. And... she spoke to me. In English."

"That is no possible. She does no speak English."

"But I could understand her. It was like..." She struggled to find the words. "She spoke to me in my head, and I could understand her. She didn't say anything, but I heard it. With my mind." She realised what she was saying made no sense, and was about to say something when Genéser cut her off.

"The Ajíngu she is most powerful. She have much powers. She can give and take knowledge, thoughts, memories. Maybe she learn English from you." Mary held onto a rock to boost herself up a particularly steep incline.

"So you're saying that she could look into my mind, find all the English that I know, and transfer it to her mind?" Mary asked, unnerved. The thought that this woman, who she didn't know, could just go poking around in her head was more than a little disquieting.

"I do not know. It is possibility."

The mountain was sliding beneath their feet, the loose fragments of stone shifting as they climbed upwards, pulling themselves over rocks, the worn path leading them ever onwards. Behind them, the sun continued to slowly rise over the rim of the horizon, the warm rays lighting their backs as they ascended.

After half an hour of scrambling as they scaled the side of the sheer cliff, Mary eventually pulled herself over a lip of rock and rolled over onto the plateau, sucking in lungfuls of air, sweat glistening on her brow from the exertion. Remarkably, she didn't feel overly hot. The tunic truly was a masterpiece of design, insulating enough to keep out the cold but light enough to prevent the wearer overheating. Next to her, Genéser rolled over the ridge to lie at her side, his great dark chest rising as falling as he caught his breath. For a moment they lay there, staring up at the slowly lightening sky, faint wisps of cloud drifting on the light breeze above. Then she sat up, and her jaw dropped.

The plateau that formed the seat of The Chair of the Goddess was flat and bare, stretching out fifty feet wide and twice as long again. The grooves worn into the rock led past where they were lying, cut across the shelf, and disappeared into the rock face.

Except it wasn't a rock face.

Two great metal doors, each one twenty feet wide and ten tall, were built into the side of the mountain, the metal surfaces weather-beaten and scratched, yet showing no signs of rust or tarnish. The rest of the mountain towered up above the doors, the rock tapering to the summit, streaks and veins of white in running down in the crevices. Mary nudged Genéser and pointed to the doors. The Mganga's eyes widened as he took in the scene before him.

"What is it?" He breathed.

"I don't know," she whispered back, not even aware that she had dropped the volume of her voice. The doors looked so alien, so out of place in the middle of the mountain, that she was still having trouble accepting that they were actually there.

Together, the pair stood up, and slowly advanced towards the metal barriers. Without quite knowing why, Mary drew the bow and nocked an arrow. Something didn't feel right about this place. It was too unnatural, to artificial. And something else. Something she couldn't quite describe, but which chilled her to her bones, which made her stomach wriggle and squirm.

"There was death here."

She looked over at Genéser, his voice startling her. "I am feel it. Many people die here." She shivered despite the tunic. He was right. A foul shadow hung over the place like a cloud, invisible but choking. This was a place that had seen violence and horror. She couldn't smell the blood or see the bodies, but she didn't need to.

She could feel it all the same.

They were closer to the doors now, the metal sheets rising up in front of them as they entered the shadow cast by the summit. As the pair stepped out of the sunlight into the shade, they were assaulted by a hideous grinding, tearing sound, so loud and close that Mary nearly dropped the bow. At the same moment, the ground beneath their feet began to shudder and rumble, the loose stones around them starting to skip and jump across the rock. It was as if the entire mountain was tearing itself apart.

The doors were opening.

As she watched, they ground slowly apart, the metal dragging and screeching over the stone. Yet the opening was entirely smooth, well-oiled machinery somewhere opening them without a shudder or pause. The door was still used, its mechanism well maintained. As the space between them grew from an inch to a foot, and then to a yard, Mary could see darkness, as black as ink, stretching out ahead. It was thick and impenetrable, even the sunlight only daring to venture a few feet in before turning back in fear. The doors continued to move, sliding apart and disappearing into the rock face, Mary was reminded of the doors beneath the Elder's bench back at the village. The chumagunuwe had come through those doors, and had almost killed her. Would the same thing happen when these opened? Would another machine come charging through to kill them both? Or would it be something even worse?

As the doors reached the final points of opening, Mary drew the bow string back, the arrow pointed into the darkness, her fingers hovering just beside her ear. Out of the corner of her eye, she saw Genéser tense, preparing for what could be about to happen.

Nothing.

The doors disappeared into the mountain, the rumbling stopped, and all was quiet.

Cautiously, Genéser stepped forward, eyes scanning the darkness for any sign of movement. He took another step, then another, until he was standing right on the threshold of the cave that had opened up ahead of them. He took one more step, carrying himself into the cavern.

Instantly, an alarm began to sound. A siren, high pitched and wailing, screeching through the air. At the same time a voice, electronic, not human, no emotion, no inflection, echoed around the empty space.

"Unrecognised lifeforms detected. Deploying security drones."

Genéser stepped back sharply, fear and surprise twisting his face. A clanking, rattling was coming from the darkness, as something, or maybe two somethings, began to move. Fast. The sound rapidly grew louder, malicious and furious in its approach until its sources burst out into the light, heading directly for the pair.

They were machines, ones that Mary had never seen before and, by the look on his face, neither had Genéser. They were pure white, made of what looked like the same metal that was woven into Mary's tunic. Six spindly legs propelled them over the stone floor, segmented bodies with swollen abdomens and thin thoraxes skimming just inches above the ground. Two waving antennae arched up from the head of each, just about the two cameras that served for eyes, the outer rims rotating as they moved to keep their targets in focus. Below the eyes, two curved mandibles protruded like scimitars, the metal gleaming wickedly as they caught the light. The two metal insects were charging at the pair, no more than twenty feet between them and their prey.

Neither of them made it to five.

Mary's arrow disappeared through the left camera of the one coming at her, the metal arrowhead piercing through the machine's armour with ease. The processing circuitry in the machine's head was completely destroyed, and it toppled forward, grinding to a halt along the ground. Mary had been aiming for its mouth, aiming to fit it between the mandibles, but even so, she was amazed she'd hit it at all. The last time she'd used a bow, it had been at a party when she was a child. But aiming and letting the arrow fly had felt surprisingly natural, as if she'd been an archer all her life.

The other had tried to leap at Genéser, jaws open, hoping to snap them together around his neck and sever his head from his shoulders. It was now lying in a smoking heap just inside the doors, part of its side melted away. Genéser's ball of fire, this one a deep grass green, hovered above the metal corpse, as if daring another to come charging from the darkness. There was a moment of silence as the two caught their breath, anticipating another attack. At last, Mary spoke.

"Why was he speaking English?"

"Who?"

"The voice. The one with the alarm."

"He was not." Genéser looked confused. "He speaks Wenyeji."

"But I could understand him. It sounded like English to me." Genéser just shook his head.

Together, they stepped over the threshold into the darkness, Mary pausing as she went to pull the arrow free from the corpse of the machine and re-nock it on the bowstring. The ball of green fire drifted ahead of them, its flickering light almost disappearing in the blackness ahead of them. As they moved further in, away from the entrance, Mary found herself being swallowed by a blackness so total that she couldn't even be sure she had eyes. The green flames barely seemed to give out any light, the few dim rays devoured hungrily by the shadows. She wanted desperately to reach out and take Genéser's hand, but she didn't dare take her hands off the bow in case they should be attacked again.

The same rumbling they'd heard when they arrived started again from behind them, and, turning around, Mary saw with horror that the great metal doors were closing again. Even as she watched, the rectangle of light that was their only glimpse of anything beyond darkness began to shrink, going from the size of a bus to a van, to a car. Then, it was snuffed out, and darkness fell.

It was only then that Mary became aware of the silence, so complete and unbroken that for a moment she was certain she'd gone deaf. She couldn't see. She couldn't hear. It was as if she'd fallen out of reality, as if she'd just suddenly ceased to exist.

Then, the ball of green fire began to blaze more strongly, pushing back the darkness, fighting to keep them in the light. Looking sideways, she could just make out the form of her companion, nothing more than a faint silhouette in the shadows. Her grip on the bow tightened. There was no going back now.

Together, they walked forwards, ears open for any sound. Mary constantly felt like she was being watched, like there were invisible eyes watching her from the darkness. The green light seemed pathetic, ineffectual, surrounded by so much black. As they made their way further and further into the heart of the mountain the air become colder and thicker, until breathing was almost like sucking in water. Mary began to feel a glowing sense of claustrophobia, of the great mass of rock baring down on them. And still the tunnel went on, the darkness extending further and further. They might have been walking for ten minutes. They could have been walking an hour. The suffocating blackness was even wiping out time. What if they never got out? What if they were doomed to wander this place forever until starvation turned them to bones and thirst dried them to leather?

She could see.

The light had been so small and faint that she almost doubted she'd even seen it. It had been there just over a second, a small burst of light, like someone lighting a match and then snuffing it out. But it had been there. She was sure of it.

"Come on." She whispered to Genéser, jumping at the sound. The gaping cavernous space had gone from wiping out noise to amplifying it, and her voice seemed startlingly loud. She hurried forwards, both hands still gripping the bow, the sound of Genéser's footsteps right behind her. The little green ball darted ahead of them, leading them ever onwards.

Another burst of light. Just as brief, but stronger, closer this time. They pressed on, running now, desperate to escape the clutches of the darkness that enveloped them. More flares, each one nearer than the last, guided their way until, at last, they could pick out metal in the dim light of the ball of fire. It was a railing, attached to a barrier. Getting closer, Mary saw that the barrier was on some sort of observation platform, the cavernous floor dropping away on the other side. The metal gleamed very faintly in another short flash, this one closer than any. Whatever was making them was on the other side of the barrier, on the floor below. Mary warily stepped towards it, Genéser at her side.

Just as she reached it, a burst of flame leapt up on the other side of the metal railing, the sudden heat and light so close that she jumped back in fear. Genéser caught her to stop her from falling.

"You are alright?"

She nodded, straightened up, and approached the barrier again. She had the bow out in front of her, the arrow still nocked on the string. Very carefully, she peered over the railing to what lay below.

Mary hadn't known what she would find inside the mountain. But she could never have imagined this.

The tunnel opened up into a massive chamber that dropped away at least thirty feet beneath them. She couldn't tell if the cavern was natural or manmade, but there were electric lights and banks of machinery built into the walls, conveyor belts and hydraulic arms, computer displays and control panels. The system was fully operational, the machinery alive and whirring as it went about whatever it had been designed to do. With a start, Mary realised what she was looking at.

It was a factory.

This was where the machines were made.

No.

They weren't being made.

She'd spotted a machine on a workbench across the cavern from her. Even with its electrical guts pulled out and its panelling hanging open, Mary would have recognised the curving silver tusks and stamping hooves anywhere. It was the chumagunuwe, the boar that had nearly killed her less than a day ago. On the belt next to it, she saw the chumarhin that had carried her to the village, its legs screwed off and lying next to it. She could just make out her reprogramming device still plugged into the side port.

It wasn't a factory. It was a repair shop.

As she was about to turn to look at Genéser, another ball of flame danced up from beneath her. She glanced down. And her heart stopped.

There were three dragons below the platform.

Actual, real, fire-breathing dragons.

Two were white, one black, their scaly hides glinting in the light. Each was at least twenty feet long, the black one easily half that again. Twisting horns curved out above the eyes, talons like kitchen knives resting on the floor. Even as she watched, the black one opened its mouth, revealing row upon row of glistening, dripping daggers, and spewed out a column of fire, straight into the open mouth of what looked like a furnace. It was only then that Mary saw the restraining shackles and straps, realised why all three looked so miserable and defeated. They were slaves, prisoners, forced to work in this place that they didn't belong.

But who was making them work?

Mary was about to ask her companion, when a slight cough from behind them made her spin around, drawing the bow as she did so.

There was a man standing behind them, arms by his sides, legs shoulder width apart. He was dressed strangely, a tight bodysuit that seemed to be made of a single piece of material. It fitted him very tightly, as if his body had been poured into the suit after it had been made. The man's face was old and lined, his hair white and wispy. But the strangest thing about him was that he seemed to be... glowing.

"You should not be here." He said. His voice was soft, and carried no threat. He sounded, if anything, a little sad.

"Who are you?" Mary said, still gripping the bow tightly.

"I'm sorry, but I don't understand your language. Although, from your face, it seems that you can understand me. How peculiar." He shrugged. "I see your friend is somewhat more local than you. Maybe he can do the talking."

Mary turned to Genéser.

"How can I understand him? He's not speaking English, is he?"

"No. He speaks Wenyeji." Genéser thought for a moment. "Hold on. I try something."

"Can you understand me, Mary?" The words she heard were in English, but his lips hadn't formed the sounds she was hearing.

"Did you just say something in Wenyeji?" She gasped. "I could understand you."

"Yes. I don't know how this happened, but I think talking is going to be a lot easier now."

The old man coughed again, drawing their attention back to him.

"Well, this is interesting-," he began, but Genéser cut him off.

"Who are you? What is this place?"

"Me? I am dead." The old man shook his head. "My name was Zeliston when I was alive, and I helped built this place. We lived hundreds of years ago, long before you and the other tribes ruled this land. As for where we are, is it not obvious? This is where the machines are repaired."

"If you're dead, how are you talking to us?"

"My consciousness was uploaded to the facility's computer mainframe after my death. I help to run the facility, keep everything working. What you're looking at right now is a hologram, I'm afraid."

"Did you make the machines?" Genéser asked. Zeliston nodded.

"We were once a great civilisation. We built great cities, developed technologies more advanced that anyone in the universe, lived in global peace and harmony for centuries. And yes, we built the machines. We wanted to leave something to continue life on this planet when, inevitably, all natural life died out. We designed them based on real animals, programmed them with such advanced artificial intelligences that they truly came to life. They were our greatest creations yet, and we built hundreds of them. Thousands. And we built this place, run by yet more machines, so that they could be repaired should they be damaged. They could go on forever, keep the planet surviving long after we were gone."

Zeliston paused, and a faint gleam of sadness crept into his eyes. "But we made a mistake. We made them too intelligent. They realised that we were their only threat and so, without hesitation, they turned on us. All of them. They attacked us out of nowhere, killing us in our thousands. They wiped us out, destroyed our cities, razed any trace of our existence."

"Then why have they not killed us?" Genéser demanded, a note of frustration rising in his tone.

"They don't yet consider your people to be advanced enough to be a threat." Zeliston raised his hand as Genéser started to indignantly open his mouth. "Please, do not mistake me. I know that you are a highly developed people. But the machines do not yet believe you are capable of eliminating all of them, as we could. That is why they have let you live. However, that is all about to change." He turned, and looked directly at Mary. "Because of you. You, and your kind."

"What?" Mary looked at the holographic man before her, unable to believe what she was hearing.

"What do you mean?" Genéser was sounding angrier and angrier, the ball of green flame glowing hotter and brighter.

"When her kind landed, bringing in their advanced technology and weaponry, the machines realised that a new threat had arrived, a dangerous one. Your people have the potential to destroy the machines, and so they will try to destroy you. They're co-ordinating as we speak. And they will not discriminate." Here he looked at Genéser. "Your people will be slaughtered as well. I'm sorry to tell you this, but there is nothing you can do. The attack will begin at sundown, and by the same time tomorrow, every single one of both your people will be dead." He looked between the two of them, genuine sorrow in his holographic eyes. "Including you two."

Mary let the arrow fly.

It passed harmlessly through Zeliston, sailing across the cavern until it struck the panel behind him. The panel where she had seen the projector creating his image. Zeliston disappeared, sparks crackling as the device was destroyed. Harsh, white lights snapped on, and an alarm began to blare at the same instant. With horror, Mary heard the sounds of metal feet falling on the stone floor in the passage from which they'd come. They were trapped, a steep drop behind them, metallic death approaching them from the front. Was this really what it had all been for? Were they really destined to just be the first to die, their people following soon after. She looked at Genéser, expecting his eyes to show fear, sadness, despair, the same emotions she was feeling.

Instead, she saw anger. Raw, uncontained anger. And determination.

He had an idea.

"Keep them busy." He snapped, hurrying past her.

"What?" Mary yelled after him.

"Buy me some time. Keep them off me." He called back, moving further along the platform. It was disorientating. She could see his lips forming words she didn't recognise, but the voice she was hearing was speaking in plain English. It was like watching a poorly dubbed film, although one with better voice acting than most.

She nocked another arrow into the bow, picked a target in the distance and let it fly. There was a thud as something crashed to the floor. But the drumming of metal on stone was still coming, getting louder and louder at an alarming rate. Whatever Genéser was doing, he'd better do it quickly. She risked a look backwards, and saw him standing on the platform, a look of intense concentration on his face. The ball of green fire had disappeared, although he was moving his hands as if he were still controlling it.

Mary fired another arrow at an approaching machine, hitting it in the front leg and making it topple into its neighbour. They were moving forwards in a solid mass, so many metallic bodies glinting in the light that looking at them was almost like looking into crystal ball. Mary continued to fire arrow after arrow at them, hitting each time, the magic charms woven into the weapons guiding her missiles straight and true. But for every machine she felled, another stepped over the corpse and carried on, the line not even braking as she desperately tried to stop their approach.

There was a hiss from just next to her, and something hurled itself at her, knocking her onto the floor, the bow falling from her fingers. It was another giant metal ant, its jaws snapping together as it strained forward, trying to bite her head off. Mary yelled out, forcing the creature up to keep it away from her face. With her free hand, she scrabbled at her waist, found the knife, yanked it free slashed upwards, aiming for the neck where she could see the wires in the metal joint. The blade passed through them effortlessly, cleaving the wires without a pause. The ant shuddered, then stilled, falling off her. Mary scrambled to her feet, searching for the bow. It was lying on the floor a few feet away, but looking up, she saw that the advancing machines were nearly upon her. She closed her eyes.

A colossal screech made them snap open again. She looked over at Genéser, who was breathing heavily, a look of triumph on his face. Before she could ask what he'd done, she saw for herself.

The black dragon, the smouldering end of the chain around its neck still dangling, rose up over the platform on its leathery wings, red eyes glowing, talons hanging beneath it as it hovered. It took one look at the crowd of approaching machines, roared in hatred, and let loose a torrent of fire, bright orange flames spewing out in a hellish river. Mary dived back to the ground, her hands over her head, desperate to avoid the flames. When the whooshing stopped, and she dared look up, all that remained of the machines were blacked, twisted shells.

The dragon shrieked with satisfaction, and dove into the tunnel, which was much wider than Mary had realised. The dragon must have had a twenty-foot wingspan, but it was easily able to glide down the passageway, wingtips not even grazing the walls.

Genéser pulled Mary to her feet, his face set in determination.

"Come on." He barked. "We've got to get out of here. We have to warn the tribe."

Mary scooped up the bow as they ran past, and the two of them raced down the passageway together, dodging around the cremated metal corpses that filled the space. While the walk into the facility might have seemed endless, the run out seemed to take even longer. Mary half believed that they were no longer running at all, that they'd died and this was some kind of torment, always running towards the entrance but never able to make it.

And then suddenly, the outside world appeared, a glowing hole melted through the metal doors that had shut them in. Genéser didn't so much as hesitate before diving through the opening, Mary close behind, doing her best to avoid touching the blistering metal. She could feel the heat coming off it as she went through. They were back on the rocky plateau, the plains stretching out beneath them. A screech drew their eyes upwards, and they saw the dragon circling the mountain above them, vividly black against the sky, which was rapidly turning orange as the sun began to set.

Sundown.

That was when Zeliston had said the attack would begin. Quickly, Mary scanned the sky around them, searching desperately for the sun. She found it, the bottom of its rim just an inch above the horizon. She guessed that they had no more than two hours, and it had taken them almost double that to walk here that morning.

"We have to go!" Genéser was already at the edge of the shelf, starting to climb down. Mary followed suit, knowing that they had a lot ground to cover if they were going help save the Wenyeji tribe.

The question was, could they do it in time?

This story was, as I'm sure some of the gamers out there will have recognised, heavily inspired by Horizon Zero Dawn, the award-winning PlayStation game. The idea of giant, mechanical, living creatures was one that captured me from the first concept, and then after I played through it, I knew I had to write about something similar. At the same time though, I wanted to inject something a little different, something mystical and spiritual into a heavily sci-fi story. After all, why should these two titans of the fictional world not come together in this way? The idea of advanced, futuristic technology set side by side with genuine, actual magic creates, at least in my opinion, a nice contrast that helps make both of them more engaging. One of the longer pieces in this book, I never actually intended for it to reach this size. But this is one of the wonderful things about writing. When you let your words run away with you, when the story develops beyond what you had initially planned, when the twists make themselves and the characters speak their own voices, that is when you know you have hit upon something special.

Time in a Bottle

The sunlight filtering in through the window falls on the vase, the curved, unblemished surface reflecting the rays in pools of white that obscure the decorative pattern. The shadow cast by the porcelain flask stains the oak surface of the side table, the darkness spilling over the edge to fall to the carpet of the alcove. The carpet is cream, recently cleaned, thick and soft enough to be comfortable without swallowing anything that treads on it. The circular alcove curves out of the side of the living room, three windows hanging like pictures on the wall, framed black and white photographs standing to attention on the windowsills. The pictures show children, grinning in the snow, thick coats speckled with white. A boy in school uniform, leather satchel slung over his shoulder, shoes brightly polished. Another shows a man and a woman, arm in arm, in formal dress, hats and jackets. Both are smiling. The man is holding a box, in which a medal, won in the war, lies on black velvet.

The vase is white, patterned with blue, sculped to evoke the body of a beautiful woman. The blue decoration shows flowers and vines, plant life twisting around the concave curves, weaving in and out of the shadows. It's no Ming relic or Ancient Greek amphora, but it holds itself with a dignified beauty that many antiques would struggle to attain. The vase is empty, more an ornament than a resting place for flowers.

Outside, a horse and trap trundles slowly past the window on the road outside, the wheels slowly rotating as the hooves rise and fall in perfect rhythm on the other side of a wrought iron fence. The fence, punctuated by great exclamation marks of stone, is topped with ornate spikes, although the time for such defences has long since passed.

A hand, wrinkled and old, clutching a duster, slowly extents towards the vase. The yellow cloth, faded from age and use, very gently rubs over the porcelain surface. The cloth travels around the back of the vase, brushing over every inch of the china. The hand lifts the vase up and inverts it, a slight shadow of dust falling onto the oak table top. This is quickly wiped up by the hand with the yellow cloth. The vase is replaced, carefully positioned in the centre of the table, where the light will catch it best. Periodically, people come into the room, usually in groups, ladies in hats and gentlemen in suits. Tea is served off the table, pleasantries are exchanged.

Now the living room is changing. The sofa is changed, leather giving way to fabric. The photos are swapped out, the children now older, smiling in black gowns instead of white snow. Blinds are installed on the windows. The dresser in the corner is removed, a leather armchair put in its place. As is the round table in the centre of the room. The walls are repapered, the flowery pattern fading to a cool cream, almost matching the carpet, one of the few things left untouched. The vase still stands on the table in the alcove. The oak surface has started to bleach in the sunlight, the deep brown slowly brightening to a pleasant chestnut.

Another pair of hands, this one younger, softer, picks up the vase, and carries it out of the room. Soon, it is returned, placed back in its position in the middle of the wooden surface. Now, a faint sloshing sound can be heard from within, and flowers are sprouting from the top like hair. Lilies, slowly opening in the sunlight, bright white stars with emerald comet tails. The living room is used more frequently, but by fewer people, spending longer periods on the sofa, or in the armchair, reading and smoking.

The room undergoes another metamorphosis, as new people enter the house even as others leave. All the photos change, the children disappearing. A smiling young man in military dress takes pride of place on the mantlepiece, although the man himself is never seen in the room. The fireplace itself is blocked up, a sheet of marble set into the wall to cover the hole. The furniture is changed again, more armchairs added, the side table replaced by a lower, lighter one, this one of pine. And atop it is placed the vase once more, its hairdo of flowers now the blond heads of nodding sunflowers.

Children, young but getting older every moment, pass in and out of the room, laughing and playing, dolls and sticks in their hands that to them become lifelong companions or pirate's cutlasses. Once, one of them gets a little too close to the table, the vase wobbling as an outstretched arm knocks it. A stern scolding is administered, although the scolder is not sure why the vase is so important.

Then the house empties.

The wallpaper peels from the walls. The carpet, unused but uncleaned, collects dust, the thick soft material filling with mites and debris as it darkens. The fabric furniture fades, as does the wood. The vase too, kept in direct sunlight, bleaches, the intricate blue embossing slowly becoming more and more translucent. The room is silent. Empty. Dead.

Until, all of a sudden, life returns.

The sound of voices, happy, filled with love, fills the house. Small feet pound up and down the stairs and along the landing. The faded sofa and armchairs are removed, leather upholstery taking their place. The wallpaper is carefully stripped, the carpet ripped up. New flooring, the material thinner and lighter, is laid down, paint meticulously administered to the walls and ceiling. A television set is mounted in the corner, a coffee table placed beside the sofa. More photos, glossy and colourful, line the windowsills and mantlepiece. The fireplace now holds an electric fire, the pokers and shovel only for decoration.

And in a small alcove sits a vase. White and faded blue, decorated with flowers. An antique. A relic. A memory of time gone by.

Although they would seem the least likely two to share a bond, there is actually a connection between Time in a Bottle and The Man Who Isn't There. Both were written for the same competition, at a time when I was experimenting with writing more descriptive pieces, trying to tell stories without using too much action. I think Time in a Bottle is one of the more pleasant pieces I've written to date. No guns, no demons, no death. Just a vase in a room in a house, watching the world go by.

Printed in Great Britain
by Amazon

39962327R00088